HEAD OVER HORSESHOES

"Katie? Where *are* you?"

"Down here with Romance."

Jenna appeared before the stall door. She was soaked, her short brown hair plastered against her head like a bathing cap.

"What are you doing here?" Katie asked.

"Me? I believe I'm supposed to be asking you that question. We were worried about you."

"Well . . ." Katie rubbed her cheek against Romance's shoulder. The mare nickered softly.

"Never mind. I get the picture. You're not in love with Matt. You're in love with his horse."

"She needs me, Jen. She's so agitated all the time, and Matt's such a jerk."

"He really could be a good rider," Jenna pointed out. "I watch him in class with her. He's just, I don't know, tense all the time."

"Well, so is she. You should have seen her act up just now when that thunder hit."

"Katie," Jenna said seriously, "you could have been hurt. I mean *badly* hurt. And if any of the teachers ever find out about you sneaking in here, well . . . let's just say I don't want to have to be around afterward to identify the body."

"I know," Katie said reluctantly. "But I hate to let her down. She needs me."

True Romance

Beth Kincaid

JOVE BOOKS, NEW YORK

SILVER CREEK RIDERS: TRUE ROMANCE

A Jove Book / published by arrangement with
the author

PRINTING HISTORY
Jove edition / November 1994

ISBN: 0-515-11489-8

A JOVE BOOK®
Jove Books are published by The Berkley Publishing Group,
200 Madison Avenue, New York, New York 10016.
JOVE and the "J" design are trademarks
belonging to Jove Publications, Inc.

PRINTED IN THE UNITED STATES OF AMERICA

10 9 8 7 6 5 4 3 2 1

1

"I believe I may be in love."

"Those eyes . . ."

"Those shoulders . . ."

"Major muscles . . ."

"Nice hindquarters, too."

Sharon Finnerty blinked wide. "Excuse me? Did I just hear that come out of the mouth of Katie Anderson, ex–Brownie of the Year?"

"Wait a minute." Katie put her hands on her hips and glared at her three friends. "*I* was talking about that new chestnut mare. Who, exactly, were you guys talking about?"

Sharon sighed. "Actually, I was talking about the *owner* of the chestnut mare."

"Me, too," Melissa Hall agreed. "You've got to admit, he *is* major league cute."

Jenna McCloud hopped off the training ring fence where the four girls were perched. "Well, I'm with

Katie," she said. "I was talking about that mare he was arguing with. I thought he was going to have to call a tow truck to get her out of that trailer."

"As the oldest member of Thoroughbred Tent," Sharon said, "I believe I have dibs on saying hi first."

"No way," Melissa said. "We'll all take a shot and may the best woman win."

Jenna groaned. "I don't see how it's possible to drool over some guy you don't even know."

"*I* was drooling over some guy's horse," Katie pointed out.

Sharon draped her arm around Melissa's shoulder. "Unlike your older tentmates, you two are simply too young to understand the ways of true romance."

"Let's see," Katie mused. "Jenna and I are twelve, Melissa's thirteen, you're fourteen . . . Yeah, I guess you *are* getting on in years, Sharon."

A loud whinny of protest filled the air. The mare was yanking on her lead rope, refusing to be led into the stable. Her owner yanked back just as hard. "Now," he commanded angrily, until at last she relented and allowed herself to be led into the unfamiliar barn.

"Poor thing," Katie said. "She looks like a nervous wreck. He really could have been a little calmer with her."

"Yeah, he wasn't exactly Mr. Patience," Sharon said, "but you have to admit he has great hair."

"Best hair of the new campers this session," Melissa agreed. "Male or female."

"Maybe you can meet him tonight," Katie suggested.

"They're having a get-acquainted dance so the new campers can meet everybody."

Jenna did a handstand, then rolled onto the grass with a sigh. "I can't believe Silver Creek's second session's starting already," she said, sighing. "Riding camp's half over."

"And we haven't even killed each other," Sharon said.

"Yet," Melissa added. "It's only the beginning of August, Sharon."

Jenna laughed. During the first session of riding camp at Silver Creek Stables, the four girls of Thoroughbred Tent had gotten off to a rough start—so rough, in fact, that the camp counselors had nicknamed them the "Thoroughbrats." It really wasn't that they didn't like each other—in fact, Katie and Jenna had been best friends since they were toddlers. It was just that they'd all had a lot on their minds those first few days of camp.

Sharon, who had been severely injured in an accident that had killed her horse, had been having a hard time adjusting to the fact that she was no longer the championship rider she'd once been. Melissa, who was one of the few African Americans at the camp, had recently moved to New York from Maryland, and was feeling isolated and lonely. Katie, who was fairly new to riding, had been nervous about being around so many more accomplished riders.

And as for herself, Jenna had been pouting (although she hated to admit it) about the fact that her family hadn't been able to afford Turbo, the beautiful chestnut gelding she'd had her heart set on purchasing. As it had turned out, Rose, the owner of Silver Creek, had decided to buy Turbo for the stables, so everything had worked out pretty well. It wasn't quite like owning him herself, of course, but since Jenna pretty much lived at the stable anyway, it was a close second.

"You know, we're not really the Thoroughbrats anymore," Jenna said, chewing on a stem of grass. "Maybe we need a new name, something with some dignity."

"How about the Silver Creek Equestrian League?" Melissa suggested.

"Not *that* dignified," Jenna said. "That sounds like a club my grandmother would belong to. You know, where they ride sidesaddle while eating those little bitty cucumber sandwiches."

"The Silver Creek Riders," Katie said.

"Hmm. Silver Creek Riders," Sharon repeated. "I like it. It's simple, elegant, makes a statement without being too bold." She shrugged. "Still, I was kind of attached to Thoroughbrats."

"Come on, Riders," Jenna said, leaping up. "Lunchtime. Rumor has it we're having beanie weenie. If you don't get in line early, you get all bean and no ween."

She dashed off in the direction of the big old lodge, then paused and turned. People said Jenna had more pep than the Energizer Bunny, and sometimes she thought it was true. It seemed like she was always waiting for the rest of the world to catch up to her.

Her three friends were staring toward the path that led to the meadow where the campers' tents were pitched. The owner of the chestnut mare was striding along the path purposefully, his bedroll in one hand, his backpack in the other.

"You three are hopeless," Jenna chided when Katie, Melissa, and Sharon caught up with her. She nudged Katie. "And what were you drooling at this time? He didn't have his horse."

Katie blushed, something she did at least a dozen times a day. "I'll bet he's got an attitude, anyway," she said. "I mean, come on, let's face it. He's got better hair than any of us."

Jenna pushed away her lunch tray with a satisfied sigh. "I hope I'm not too full for softball," she said. "There's a game during optional." "Optional" was shorthand for the period of afternoon optional activities at Silver Creek, the time when the horses were allowed to rest up after morning lessons. "It's guys against girls," she added. "I'm pitching, Sharon's umping."

Sharon nodded at the braces on her lower legs. "I think I've found my true calling. It'd take me an hour to make it around the bases, but I can call somebody out in a split second."

"Just as long as it's a guy you're calling out," Jenna warned.

Sharon held up her hands. "Hey, I am utterly impartial. I calls 'em as I sees 'em."

Jenna slid off the wooden bench and reached for her tray. "No problemo. I'm planning on pitching a no-hitter, anyway."

"You really need to work on that self-esteem," Sharon

teased. She turned to Melissa, who was tracing fork paths through her untouched applesauce. "You coming, Melissa? You're our best left fielder."

"She's our only left fielder," Jenna pointed out.

"Sorry, No-hit," Melissa said. "I'm going to write Marcus." She frowned, her dark almond eyes someplace far away. "I haven't heard from him in four whole days."

"Don't worry, Melissa," Katie said. "I'm sure there'll be a diskette from Marcus today." Melissa and her boyfriend in Maryland wrote back and forth to each other on computer diskettes.

"How about you, Katie?" Sharon asked.

"Me? Butterfingers?" Katie laughed. She was convinced her arms and legs had been wired to her brain incorrectly. "I'm going to the art studio, where I can't hurt anyone."

She watched as Jenna and Sharon headed off together. Sharon moved with an awkward, lurching motion, but Katie barely noticed it anymore. "Sharon really seems better, don't you think?" she mused.

"Hmm?" Melissa asked distractedly.

"Sharon."

Melissa followed Katie's gaze. "She does seem happier, doesn't she?"

"Of course, I can still see how frustrated she gets in class sometimes," Katie said. "You can tell she's thinking, *I was on my way to the Olympic Equestrian Team, and now I can't post at a slow trot*. But she jokes a lot more, and she seems more relaxed."

Melissa picked up her tray and stood. "I gotta go hit the old laptop," she said.

"You're not . . . worried about anything, are you, Melissa?"

"Anything?" Melissa repeated. "You mean like Marcus anything?" She shrugged. "I guess not. When my parents divorced and my mom and I moved here, I knew it would be hard to stay close to Marcus, but I still think we can make it work. He's even been talking about coming here for a visit, wouldn't that be great? I told him he should come for the camp horse show."

"Don't remind me," Katie said. "I can't stand that word."

"Horse?" Melissa teased.

"You know which word." Katie sighed. "You and Jenna are so much better at riding than I am. And Sharon—well, she used to plaster her walls with ribbons. Me, I hate competing at things. Come to think of it, I hate tests of any kind. I mean, I panicked when I had my eyes examined."

Melissa laughed. "Katie, you've only been riding a few months. Jenna and Sharon and I have ridden for years. You'll be fine."

Katie stared at the remains of her lunch. It was easy for Melissa to be so confident. She was a straight-A, Honor Society, cheerleader, best-at-everything-she-tried kind of person. Well, sometimes second-best. She'd been reserve champion to Sharon's champion at the prestigious New England Classic Horse Show a couple years ago, back before Sharon's accident. But that was the rare exception.

"I don't know," Katie said. "I think maybe I'll wait till next year before I start doing shows. There are so

many things I still need to work on. My transitions,
my posting, my form—"

"Hey, I'm *still* working on all those things. That's
the fun of riding. You can always improve." Melissa
nodded toward the door. "I gotta go. True love and all
that. Think I'll check the mail again, just in case." She
gave Katie a melancholy smile and began to weave her
way through the thinning lunchtime crowd.

Poor Melissa. Sometimes Katie wondered whether
having a boyfriend would really be worth all the trouble. Jenna said Katie was an incurable romantic—
and it was true, she'd read plenty of teen romances.
But in books, it was always so easy. The guy took
your hand and your eyes met and the violins started
playing. No sweaty palms, no awkward silences. And
no unanswered letters, she thought, watching Melissa
walk out the door.

The art studio was a two-story frame house that had
once served as a residence for farmhands, back when
Silver Creek had been a working farm. The property
was the perfect place for the stable, Katie decided as
she made her way there through the dappled afternoon sunlight. Situated right next to a pristine state
park in upstate New York, Silver Creek owned one
hundred and forty acres of land—beautiful rolling pasture with plenty left over for cross-country treks. The
riding camp's tents were pitched right on the edge of
a lake, and Silver Creek's crystal waters meandered
through the property in graceful arcs.

A gentle piano concerto met her ears as she entered
the studio. Jay, the counselor in charge of the art

classes, always had his CD player going. Bach, Katie knew. Her stepmother, Rae, was a classical music buff.

As usual, everyone seemed to be working on the same subject. There were horse watercolors. Horse sculptures. Horse pastels. Even a horse macrame wall hanging. (At least Katie thought it was a horse. It might have been a poodle with a saddle.)

Katie smiled. It wasn't as if they didn't get enough exposure to horses. For the last month, they'd lived and breathed and dreamed them.

"Hey, Katie," Jay called from a worktable. "I've got a fresh batch of balsa wood for sculpting. Feeling brave?"

"I've kind of grown attached to all my fingers."

"Delia's upstairs teaching origami. You know, Japanese paper folding?"

"I tried a class with her the other day. All my birds looked like horses, and all my horses looked like birds." She reached for a large sketch pad on a shelf. "I think I'll stick to sketching," she added, grabbing a couple of charcoal pencils.

"What's the subject?"

"I've got somebody new in mind," Katie said. "A beautiful redhead. I'm going to work outside today."

Jay followed her out onto the porch. "Know what?" he said. "Rose told me she wants to use one of your sketches for the cover of the show programs."

"Really?" Katie cried. Rose was the owner of Silver Creek, a slightly gruff but thoroughly sweet older woman who had opened the stable when she got tired of working at the racetrack.

"She says she thinks you have a lot of talent, and believe you me, nobody's seen more horse pictures than Rose, after all these years of running Silver Creek. She likes that one you did of Blooper galloping through a pasture. She thinks you captured the real Bloop."

Katie walked toward the stable, feeling a strange mix of pride and anxiety. She was flattered that Rose liked her work enough to use it on the show program. But the very mention of the show set her stomach into a spin cycle.

She headed into the old stable and inhaled the sweet scent of hay and horse and leather. In the last stall, she saw her subject—the beautiful chestnut mare they'd watched earlier. But first she slipped inside the stall next door and knelt down next to Say-So, a sweet-tempered bay gelding. During a trail overnight while Katie had been riding him, he'd reinjured an old sprain when he'd panicked at a snake crossing his path. Fortunately, although he couldn't be ridden for a while, Say hadn't been badly hurt. The only thing in real danger of permanent injury had been Katie's ego. She'd taken a bad fall, but Sharon, using a mixture of experience and blunt sympathy, had helped her realize that it wasn't the end of the world.

"Looking good, Say," she said, give him a tender pat.

Just then Katie heard someone striding purposefully down the aisle. She glanced up in time to see the new mare's owner pass by, the great-eyes-great-hair-I-have-dibs guy Melissa and Sharon had been gaping at. Frankly, close up, Katie didn't get it. With that scowl on his face, it was hard to see what they'd been so excited about.

"You and I need to talk," he said to the mare. Katie stayed close to Say-So—not exactly hiding, but not exactly visible either.

In the next stall, the mare pricked up her ears and pranced over eagerly to greet her owner. He stared at her in annoyance. She nudged him with her muzzle, hoping for some affection.

"You really embarrassed me today, you know?" he muttered. "What was the deal with the trailer this morning? It took me an hour to get you loaded before we left. How many times have I—" Just then, Katie dropped her sketch pad. "Is somebody in that stall?" he demanded.

"I, um, I wasn't eavesdropping," Katie tried to explain, her cheeks heating up like burners on a stove. She retrieved her sketch pad and slipped out of Say-So's stall. Standing this close to the mare's owner, he seemed much taller than he had from a safe distance. Tall enough to make Katie back up a step. There was something intimidating about that dark glare of his.

"I was just checking this gelding's leg . . . He hurt it a while back and . . . well, that's sort of a long story." She nodded at his horse. "She's a beautiful mare. What's her name?"

"Romance."

"Pretty name. I'm Katie Anderson."

The guy didn't answer. He stared at Romance, an annoyed expression on his face, as if Katie had evaporated. He had intense, nearly black eyes and longish, wavy hair the same color. Sharon was right about that, at least. He *did* have nice hair.

"Well—" Katie began.

"Oh," he said, "sorry about that. I was thinking about Romance. My name's Matt Collier."

He stretched out his hand to stroke Romance's left ear. She responded eagerly, nodding her head gently to increase the pressure.

"That's enough for you," Matt said, withdrawing his hand. "After the way you embarrassed me with the trailer."

"Did you have trouble loading her?" Katie asked.

"I *always* have trouble loading her. It's the same thing every time. She stares at me for half an hour like *No WAY am I going in there.* I end up furious, and pretty soon it takes twenty people to get her loaded."

"Did you try bribing her with some grain?"

"Believe me, I've heard every trick ever invented. Bribe her. Blindfold her. Let her watch another horse load and unload. Poke at her with a broom." He sighed. "It's just her. Romance has a mind of her own. She's stubborn as a mule, and let's face it, they're real close relatives."

Katie laughed. Matt smiled for just a split second, long enough to soften that get-outta-my-way look. But a moment later the scowl returned.

"What's the paper for?" he asked, not sounding like he much cared.

Katie looked down at her sketch pad. "I was going to, um, sketch your mare, I mean, that is, if you don't mind."

"I do mind. A lot."

Katie blinked. Had she heard him right? She'd sketched almost all the other horses at Silver Creek, and people were always asking her if they could have a picture. It had never occurred to her that Matt might actually *mind* if she sketched his horse.

"Maybe you don't understand," Katie began. "I mean, it's not like I want to ride her. All I would do is spend an hour or two in her stall—"

"No!" Matt rubbed his forehead and sighed. "No," he repeated more gently. "This horse is enough trouble without you or anyone else making things more difficult. Got it?"

"Okay." Katie took a step back, holding up her palm. "Okay, I got it."

"As for you," Matt turned back to Romance, "try to behave for a change."

He charged past Katie and out the barn door, a dark silhouette against a blaze of white sun.

Katie looked at Romance. The pretty mare was weaving back and forth, her delicate features clouded by confusion and hurt, her ears flicking warily.

With a furtive glance at the barn door, Katie slipped closer to Romance's stall and held out her hand. The mare reveled in her tender strokes like a thirsty animal deprived of water.

"It's okay, girl," Katie whispered. "Don't worry about that grouch. You're going to be okay. You have me on your side now."

2

Sharon moved down the path from the softball diamond as fast as her braces would allow. Gary Stone, the local vet who cared for Silver Creek's horses, was already climbing into his pickup, and she was afraid she was going to miss him.

"Gary!" she called, but her voice was lost in the rumble of his truck motor.

She put two fingers to her lips and let out an ear-piercing whistle. Gary turned in her direction and she held up her index finger to indicate she wanted him to wait.

She rushed to him, nearly tripping on a tree root in her hurry. She hated it when people had to wait for her. It was the same frustrated feeling she got when she was riding and she couldn't get her legs to obey her brain. She could feel the eyes boring into her, could practically hear the pitying thoughts. *Poor thing, with those legs, and she used to be such a great rider, too.*

She smiled self-consciously at Gary and he smiled back, a big overgrown-kid kind of grin. Maybe he wasn't feeling sorry for her, after all. Her friends said she was way too self-conscious about the braces. If anything, Jenna liked to point out, the first thing people noticed about Sharon was her wild auburn hair with a mind of its own.

"Hey. Sharon, right?" Gary said when she was within earshot. Because Gary's wife, Margaret, was a riding teacher at Silver Creek, he knew most of the campers by name.

"Thanks for waiting," Sharon said. "I'd been meaning to catch up with you, but I kind of got bogged down umping." She jerked her head toward the softball diamond.

"Who's winning?"

"The guys are getting slaughtered. Twenty-nine–six when I left."

"You don't have to gloat."

"Listen," Sharon said, "I'm sure you're busy, but I wondered if you could take a quick look at Luna. I'm worried about her."

"Luna?" Gary frowned. "Is that the dapple gray filly?"

Sharon nodded. "Claire volunteered to lunge-train her this summer for a friend of hers. Only at the last minute she got tied up with extra work and volunteered me to do it instead. Sucker that I am."

At first, Sharon had balked at the idea of helping

with Luna. Just because her legs weren't quite up to par didn't mean she wanted to help Claire with some bratty, poorly trained filly as a consolation prize. But over time, Sharon and Luna had started to reach an understanding. Sharon wasn't a champion anymore, and Luna might never be one, but they'd developed a tentative friendship.

Gary grabbed his vet bag and stepped out of the truck. "What's wrong with this filly?"

"Well, I'm not exactly sure," Sharon admitted as they walked toward the stable. "I've only known her since camp started. She was badly trained by her original owner, and she's always been really skittish around people. But with me, once we developed an understanding, she sort of blossomed. Until a few days ago, I really felt like we were beginning to make some progress."

They stepped into the quiet shade of the stable. "What happened a few days ago?"

Sharon paused in front of Luna's stall. "Hey, Lunatic," she said. Luna looked up vaguely, her dark eyes dull. "See for yourself. She's gone off her feed, she's listless, she won't respond at all when I work with her. Just generally bummed."

"Bummed, eh?" Gary opened Luna's stall door. "I don't remember covering that in vet school." He approached Luna slowly, stroking her silvery neck. "Let's take a look at you, girl."

"The weird thing is, she can be really animated, too. I mean, she'll pace around her stall in circles like a maniac. And Kirk, one of our stablehands, told me he saw her the other day out in the west paddock, dashing back and forth along the fence for hours."

She watched while Gary took Luna's temperature and checked the filly's pulse by placing his fingers under Luna's jawbone.

"Forty-one beats per minute," he reported. "A little fast, but then, she may be a tad annoyed at the thermometer."

"Can you blame her?" Sharon asked, running her fingers through Luna's silky mane.

Gary read the thermometer. "One hundred point five. So far, so good." He reached for the stethoscope, and while he checked Luna's heart and lungs, Sharon cooed softly to the filly.

Gary was a fine vet, and a nice guy, too. With his faded jeans and unruly hair, he didn't exactly look the part of the stern physician, but Sharon had had enough of doctors to last a lifetime. She couldn't see a stethoscope without flashing back to her long, dark months in the hospital after the accident, the accident that had killed her horse Cassidy and left Sharon a shadow of the rider she'd once been.

After Gary had completed his exam, he leaned back against the wall, arms crossed over his chest. "I'm not finding any obvious pathology," he said, shaking his head. He looked over at Sharon. "Sorry, that's medical-ese for—"

"I know. I've seen my share of doctors. You mean you can't see anything obviously wrong."

"Any changes in the routine lately? Different feed? Different schedule?"

"Nope. I work with her every day on the lunge line. So does Claire, whenever she can. Luna spends most of her day out in the paddock, partying with the other horses who aren't being used in classes." She stroked Luna's velvety muzzle. "Tough life, huh?"

"Tell you what." Gary put his stethoscope in his bag. "Keep an eye on her, and give me a call if you notice any changes."

"Take two aspirin and call me in the morning," Sharon muttered.

"You know, Sharon, sometimes the problem's not physical. Horses are very sensitive. Could be she's going through a delayed reaction to being separated from her old owner."

"But she's been fine all month," Sharon said, more irritably than she'd intended. She sighed. "Sorry, Gary. I guess I just feel frustrated because I can tell *some*thing's bothering her. And I don't know why, but I feel like I'm responsible for her, you know?"

Gary smiled reassuringly. "I'm sure she'll be fine. I'll be back to check on Say-So in a few days, and I'll take another look at ol' Luna then."

"How's Say doing, anyway?"

"He'll be ready to ride by next week," Gary said.

Sharon laughed. "Which is more than I can say for Luna. We're still working on that complex concept known as *whoa*."

"I'll see you in a few days, then," Gary said.

Sharon watched him head out into the bright afternoon sunlight, feeling vaguely frustrated. She knew it wasn't Gary's fault he couldn't discover what was wrong with Luna, but sometimes it seemed like medical types never had the real answer when you needed it. It had been a doctor who'd told her she'd never leave a wheelchair again. Ever since then, Sharon had made it a point not to trust the experts.

She ran her hand in soothing strokes along Luna's back. "You know, Luna," she said, "caring for horses would be a whole lot easier if you guys would just learn to speak English." Luna looked at her with doleful eyes. "Hey, don't worry," Sharon said. "You don't speak English, but I know a few words of Horse. And one way or another, I'm going to figure out what's bothering you."

"Swing your partner, do-si-do!"

Katie locked elbows with Jim Jackson, a short, squat sixth grader, and swung around in a wild circle.

"Allemande left!" Ethan Parrish, one of the counselors, was serving as the square dance caller for the evening's festivities. And he was doing a pretty fair job, Katie thought. Not that she had much experience. The only other time she'd square danced was in gym class, when she and Jenna had been partners and they'd giggled so hard they'd been exiled to the bleachers.

When the dance was over, Katie started back to her friends, who were sitting on a bale of hay, watching the proceedings. Katie waved to Rose as she passed. The staff had really outdone themselves tonight. They'd held all kinds of special events in the evenings, but this square dance was one of their more ingenious ideas. Rose had hired a fiddler to supply the music, and there was plenty of apple cider and great food.

A team of horses pulled an old wagon around the perimeter of the camp for hay rides. The counselors had even strung thousands of little white lights in the trees. Every time the big pines swayed, the lights moved like giant swarms of fireflies.

Katie sat down next to Sharon on the last few inches of hay, feeling flushed and a little guilty. No one else seemed to be having as much fun.

"How come you guys sat out the dance?" Katie asked.

"I guess I didn't feel like it," Melissa said.

Jenna held up a paper plate with a few crumbs on it. "I wanted to try the pumpkin pie. Not bad, either."

"My legs have this way of allemanding right when they're supposed to be allemanding left," Sharon said with a good-natured laugh. "Besides, there aren't enough guys."

"Before Jim, I danced the last two with Louisa Tisch," Katie said. "You have to keep an open mind about your partner."

"I was holding out for the new guy over there," Sharon said, nodding.

Katie followed her gaze. Matt Collier was leaning against an oak in a dark spot at the edge of the clearing, a cup of cider in his hand, a frown on his face.

"But I guess he's not the do-si-do type," Sharon concluded.

"I'm kind of worried about his horse," Katie said. "I ran into him this afternoon in the stables, and he was really grouchy with her, poor thing." She sighed. "He told me not to go near her, but I just have the feeling she needs somebody, you know? Something about the way she looked at me. Crazy, I know."

"Not so crazy," Sharon said.

"Have you ever had that kind of psychic link with an animal?" Katie asked.

"With Cassidy," Sharon said wistfully.

"I have that with Turbo," Jenna added. She grinned deviously. "But you sure it's not the animal's *owner* you've got a psychic link with?"

Katie groaned. "Please."

As the fiddler put away his violin, some of the counselors began setting up a pair of speakers. "Time for some real music," Sharon said.

"I hope Rose and Claire didn't make the selections," Jenna groaned. Rose and her daughter were in charge of selecting the music that blared over the loudspeaker each morning to wake the campers. They had very odd taste in music. Sometimes it was old rock hits or TV theme songs. Once it had been the jingle for a dog food commercial.

"Here it comes," Jenna said as Claire passed by, a dark-haired, younger version of Rose. Like most of the other teachers and counselors, she was wearing a straw hat and a red bandanna around her neck. "I'm guessing it's Claire's CD of the world's greatest disco hits."

"I heard that, McCloud," Claire said. "Thanks for giving me a great idea for tomorrow's wake-up."

Minutes later a slow dance came on, filling the night air with a familiar, soulful tune. A few adventuresome high school couples began to dance, but most people just looked embarrassed.

"Hey, Melissa," Katie said. "Did you hear from Marcus?"

Melissa shook her head glumly. "Nothing."

"Tomorrow, for sure," Katie said encouragingly.

"You know, Melissa," Sharon said as she stood to adjust one of her braces, "you could ask someone to dance. Then you could write Marcus about it and make him insanely jealous."

"Right, Sharon. Not in this universe."

"It's easy," Sharon said, tossing back her hair. "Nothing to it. I've even asked guys out before."

"Sure, Sharon." Jenna rolled her eyes. "You talk big, but how many?"

"Dozens. Well, okay. Maybe not dozens. Maybe more like one." Sharon paused. "And he was my cousin and we were just going to a movie, but still. The principle's the same."

Katie noticed a guy named Adam leaning against a tree behind Sharon, listening intently. She recognized him as a counselor, a sophomore who also took lessons in the winter at Silver Creek. Katie started to signal Sharon that she had an observer, but Jenna gave her a conspiratorial don't-tell smile.

"So how exactly *do* you ask a guy to dance, Sharon?" Katie asked innocently.

"Simple. Smile. Walk right on up. Don't beat around the bush. I mean, he'll either say yes or no, right? So why not just get it over with? It's only fair." Sharon shrugged. "Why should guys be the only ones to go through the humiliation of hearing *no, thanks*? These are the nineties, girls. Fair is fair. You just march on up and say, 'Excuse me, would you like to dance?' "

Adam stepped forward and tapped Sharon on the shoulder. "Glad to."

Sharon spun around, nearly losing her balance. "Oh. No. I was just . . . I was just asking hypothetically."

"Okay, then. I'd be glad to hypothetically dance."

"No, really. I didn't mean—" Sharon looked over at her friends helplessly.

"She talks big, but she's pure chicken," Jenna commented.

"Kentucky Fried," Katie agreed.

Melissa made a clucking noise.

Adam held out his hand. "Come on. You stall any longer, the song will be over."

"I guess you saw through my strategy." Sharon sighed. "Look. I mean, *really* look. See the braces? I can't dance."

"What a coincidence." Adam pulled her toward the open area where several couples were swaying gently. "I can't either."

They began to move, very slowly and stiffly, to the music. "Aww," Jenna said. "This is so romantic."

Romance. Suddenly Katie jumped to her feet. "I've got something I need to do at the stable."

"I'll go with you," Jenna offered.

"That's okay. I'll just be a minute. I think I left my jacket there when we were cleaning tack this morning." It wasn't a complete lie. She'd left her jacket there the day before yesterday.

"Hurry," Jenna urged. "You don't want to miss the next installment of the Young and the Rhythmless."

Halfway down the path, Katie paused and checked behind her. Matt was leaning against the tree, watching the festivities. Sharon and Adam were still swaying back and forth, more or less in time to the music.

Katie smiled. They could have their romance. She had one of her own in mind.

Katie eased the big barn door open a few inches and slipped into the stable. The lights were off, but moonlight streamed through the windows over the doors. If only she could paint this scene. All the usual daytime sights—horses peering expectantly over their doors, stablehands coming and going, riders carrying grooming tools or tack—had vanished. The whole barn had been drained of color. Everything was light and shadow, frosted with the silvery sheen of moonlight like a dusting of chalk.

Katie tiptoed down the aisle toward Romance's stall. As the horses heard her, most perked up expectantly. Who was this late-night visitor, lurking in their midst? Could this mean food? A midnight ride? A late-night muzzle scratch?

Katie loved to imagine what was going on inside the minds of animals, especially horses. Rose said she was part horse, she had such good instincts. If her grades were good enough, Katie hoped someday to become a veterinarian at a zoo, maybe working to help breed endangered species. Sometimes she wondered how likely that would be, though. She wasn't like her older brother and sisters, John and Natalie and Elise. John, a sophomore at Harvard. Nat, a senior in high school with an A-plus average, well on her way to becoming valedictorian. And Elise, a junior at fifteen who'd skipped eighth grade because she was "bored." Sometimes Katie secretly wondered if she'd been adopted. Even Beauty, the family mutt, had graduated from obedience school at the top of his class.

Near the end of the long row of stalls, Romance was waiting for her, her regal head turned hopefully in Katie's direction, ears pricked expectantly. "Romance," Katie whispered as she opened the stall door. "Hi, sweet girl."

She reached up to stroke the mare's neck, and Romance seemed to devour the attention, eagerly dipping her head, her eyes glazed with moonlight and a look of pure delight.

A second later, however, she was devouring *Katie*. First she tried to chew a lock of Katie's hair. "No, silly girl," Katie said firmly, but Romance pressed on, nibbling at Katie's shirt collar.

Katie yanked it free, rolling her eyes. Romance looked at her reproachfully.

"I know you're not hungry," Katie chided. "Besides, polyester is not one of the four basic food groups."

In the moonlight the mare's chestnut coat turned the color of an old, tarnished penny. She wasn't a big horse, maybe fourteen or fifteen hands, but there was something breathtaking about her strength. You could see it in the sinewy strength of her legs and her strong, compact back. But it was her eyes that mesmerized Katie, prominent, expressive, wide-set. Did she have a touch of Arabian in her? Probably, although Katie didn't know enough about the breed to be certain.

Still, she knew enough to have fallen head over heels with Romance. *Why?* she wondered. After all, she loved all of Silver Creek's horses. For that matter, she loved her menagerie at home—Beauty and Beast, her dog and cat; her assorted gerbils; her blind lizard, Charlie; and her tarantula, Charlotte, who had a fondness for corn dogs. She loved just about everything in the animal kingdom, with the possible exception of roaches and those wicked-looking scorpion things you found in the desert.

She thought she heard steps outside and froze. But after a few seconds, she decided it was just the trees next to the stable, scraping against the old wooden structure. Still, she knew she should be going. Jenna would come looking for her soon. And if Matt found her here . . . well, he didn't sound like he wanted anyone within a hundred feet of Romance. She had the feeling she didn't want to be on the receiving end of his temper.

Katie reached into her jeans pocket, where she found a slightly gooey sugar cube. She held it out in her palm and Romance practically inhaled it.

"Remind me to teach you some table manners," she remarked as Romance nudged her hand for more.

"Sorry, that's all," Katie explained. She scratched Romance's ear to distract her from the subject of sugar, but Romance wasn't about to be deterred that easily. She pawed the ground, swishing her tail impatiently, then pushed at Katie's shoulder with her muzzle.

Katie held up her hands. "See? No more, I'm telling you. I'm really not holding out."

She knew there were two schools of thought on giving horses treats. Some people claimed that it made them nippy and ill-mannered. Others said that when used judiciously with the right horses, food could reinforce positive behavior and be helpful as an occasional treat.

Katie had thought Romance seemed like a prime candidate for a treat or two, but now she wasn't so sure, as Romance pushed at Katie in the darkness, using her powerful shoulder to muscle her into a corner of the stall.

For a brief moment, Katie panicked. A horse was a massive, incredibly strong animal, and this was a horse she didn't really know. She was here all alone in this dark barn. A kick from one of Romance's powerful hind legs, and Katie could be a mass of broken bones.

Get a grip, she told herself. She pushed back against Romance's shoulder. Romance pushed back harder, forcing Katie up against the automatic waterer in the corner.

She could see the headlines in the *Silver Creek Gazette*: GIRL, 12, FOUND FLATTENED. SUSPECT MARE IN CUSTODY.

Romance pawed the ground, thrashing her head up and down. Katie couldn't be sure in the darkness, but she seemed to be gloating.

Katie knew she couldn't let the mare have the upper

hand. She put her hands on her hips in a gesture of firmness. "No, Romance," she said, mustering her most threatening voice. Katie stood on tiptoe, trying to look bigger. "No," she said again.

Romance considered for a split second, then backed up two steps.

"That's more like it. You were very rude," Katie scolded.

Romance's dark eyes filled with moonlight, like cream in coffee. She held her head to one side, nodding gently to show she was sorry. At least that's what Katie wanted to believe she meant.

Katie slipped out of the corner and draped her arm around Romance's neck. She was just a big baby, that was all. Alone in a new place, with a grouch for an owner. You had to forgive her for being a little grouchy herself, didn't you?

Katie rubbed her cheek on the mare's smooth-as-silk mane. "I'll come back, I promise," she said. "But don't tell anyone, okay? It'll be our little secret."

She sneaked back out of the barn, sliding the door shut. Laughter floated on the breeze. Katie could just make out the strains of a tune that she recognized from the radio. *I'll be there for you 'cause I care for you,* went the song.

She would be there for Romance, in spite of Matt— or maybe *because* of him. Romance needed her, Katie was sure of it. She couldn't explain it if she tried. She just *knew*.

She walked back to the dance, humming softly to

herself. She would tell Jenna she couldn't find her jacket. But she wouldn't say a word about her visit with Romance. It would be her secret for the rest of the session, and no one would ever have to know. No one but Romance.

3

"Now, before we cool down the horses, let's work on those circles one more time. First a walk, then a rising trot." Margaret Stone stood at the edge of the training ring, shielding her eyes from the sun with her right hand. "Remember that if you're using your aids correctly, the bend in your horse's body all the way from poll to tail will mirror the arc of the circle. Use your outside leg just behind the girth to keep your mount's hindquarters from swinging out. Use your inside leg to maintain impulsion and control the amount of bend."

Sharon gave Escape Route a pat. *Easier said than done*, she thought, not that it was 'Cape's fault. He was a rawboned gelding Rose had rescued from being put down, a bay with a white muzzle and a sweet temper. Despite his age, he was a good ol' guy, just perfect for Sharon. In the old days, before her accident, she would have dozed off on a horse as docile as Escape Route. These days, with her leg muscles still weak and unreliable, it was all she could do to handle him.

"Let's start with a walk, one at a time so I can really get a look at you. Remember, never ask a horse to turn with your hands alone. You're going to end up turning the forehand of the horse, while the caboose—that's what one of my beginner riders calls the hindquarters— is going to end up faring for itself. The result will be a very sloppy turn. So use those legs." Margaret gazed at the class. There were several new faces this session. "Sharon," she called, "why don't you start us off?"

Sharon nudged Escape into a walk and began to trace a fairly tight circle, large enough for Escape to walk comfortably. She didn't need to think about Margaret's instructions. She'd ridden so long they might as well have been permanently wired into her brain. But her left leg was still weak, and her right wasn't much stronger. And that made using her leg aids a definite challenge.

Well, she was just going to have to compensate as best she could. She turned her hips in the direction of the bend so they were roughly parallel with Escape's hips. She used her inside hand to lightly guide him into the bend. She rotated her shoulders and upper body a bit.

Then she summoned up all her strength and will- power and *commanded* her legs to obey her. At least for one complete circle.

"Nice work, Sharon," Margaret called.

Sharon smiled with pleasure, then caught herself. There had been a time when she could have done this exercise in her sleep. Of course, that was then, and this was now. And there was nothing wrong with being proud of herself, even if it was for something as simple as a nicely executed circle.

When she was finished, she rode to the edge of the group. Margaret called Katie next. Katie had improved a lot during the first session of camp, Sharon decided as she watched her friend trace the same circle. She wasn't a natural rider, the way Melissa was—or Jenna could be, when she wasn't showing off—but she was a sensitive rider. She definitely had a lot of potential.

"You know, you've really gotten better since camp started, Katie," Sharon said as Katie walked Blooper over to join Sharon and Escape Route.

"Really?" Katie asked, practically glowing.

"When you learn to be a little stronger with the horse, you'll be onto something," Sharon said. "Sometimes you have to let him know who's boss."

"I think you've improved, too," Katie said. "Not, of course, that I'm exactly the expert, but—"

"No," Sharon interrupted. "You can tell a lot, just from watching someone. I have to admit, I'd planned to be back to my old form by the end of the summer, and now it's pretty obvious there's no danger of that. Remember how mad I was about being placed in this class? Now I'm just happy when I can dismount without landing on my . . . uh, dignity."

"Come on," Katie chided as she reached down to stroke Blooper's neck, "you've made amazing progress. Not to mention all the progress you've made with Luna."

Sharon frowned. "Actually, we haven't made much

progress at all, not lately. I asked Gary to look her over yesterday, and he said she seemed fine, but still, I have the feeling something's bothering that filly. That reminds me. I was going to go over and check on her in the west paddock, to see if everything's okay over there. Kirk said everything was fine, but . . . well, I'm running out of options. Want to ride over with me?"

"Sure," Katie said. "Let's ask Margaret."

As soon as class was over and they had the go-ahead from Margaret, the girls rode down the long, winding path that led away from the rings to the large paddock where many of the Silver Creek horses grazed. They walked at a leisurely pace, enjoying the sun on their backs while they allowed the horses to cool down after their workout in class.

It surprised Sharon, how much she'd grown to love gentle rides like this, at a walk or a casual trot. With Cassidy, she'd always been thinking big—the next wild gallop, the next tough jump course, the next big show.

Now she was learning to enjoy the gentle loll of 'Cape's gaits, to be pleased when her tight-as-a-stretched-rubber-band muscles loosened just a bit, or to take in the wildflowers growing carelessly by the side of the road. Shows didn't take up a lot of her mind anymore. Maybe, just maybe, they never would again.

"I'm not going to enter the camp show." Sharon surprised herself by saying it out loud.

"You're not?" Katie asked calmly. Sharon had expected her to argue, or at least to be a little shocked.

Escape Route paused to eat a dandelion, and although Sharon knew she shouldn't let him run the show, she allowed him to munch away. "I just . . ." Her voice trailed off. "I don't know. Partly, I'm not ready. I could only enter the really basic kiddie stuff. Walk/trot, maybe."

Katie drew Blooper to a halt. "Like me," she said with a self-deprecating smile.

"It's different with you, Katie. You're a new rider. I'm . . . I'm an old new rider. A new old rider."

"I understand," Katie said as they picked up their walk again. "You won the championship at the New England Classic, Sharon. You don't have anything to prove."

"It's not that, either. It's like I'm learning to ride all over again, not for the competitive thing, which is what I used to live for, let's face it. This time I'm learning to ride for the sake of riding."

"Maybe I won't enter, either," Katie said thoughtfully. "Rose said no one had to. And the truth is, I hate competitive things. I freeze up. I guess I'm the exact opposite of you that way."

"Yeah," Sharon said wistfully. "I love that whole adrenaline rush of trying to be the best."

"You'd fit right into my family," Katie said. "They're incredibly competitive. I used to hate to play Monopoly with them on Sunday afternoons. It was like World War Three every time."

Sharon pointed to a big elm tree near the white post and rail fence that encircled the huge paddock. They rode over and stopped near the fence in the cool shade of the tree.

"Well, a show isn't just about competition," Sharon pointed out. She gazed across the open green meadow. Luna was nowhere in sight, but three other camp horses were frolicking like children at recess. "It's a way to monitor your progress, to compare you and your horse to other riders your same skill level. It's really a good way to learn, Katie. And this camp show's just for fun. Very low-key. No pressure."

"Easy for you to say. You're not going to enter."

"Do as I say, not as I do." Sharon grinned. "Hey, you want to talk pressure?" She paused to watch as Foxy, a piebald mare, and Jenkins, a gray mare, began an elaborate game of horse tag.

"Those two are always hanging out together," Katie remarked. "Isn't it funny the way horses make buddies with each other?" She turned to Sharon. "So what were you saying? About pressure?"

"Oh. You know Adam? That guy I danced with last night?"

"I believe you mean *that guy I danced with three times last night.*"

"Brave soul. Well, anyway, he knows Matt Collier, the guy you ran into in the stables with the great hair and the pretty chestnut."

"Romance."

"Well, he *is* cute, but—"

"No. Romance is the name of his mare."

Sharon laughed. "Well, it turns out Adam and Matt went to a different camp last summer, one in the Berkshires. They didn't like it, thought it was sort of snobby, and that's why they both applied here at Silver Creek. Anyway, Matt's older brother is a great rider, according to Adam. You know, hundreds of ribbons and trophies, could even be ranked nationally someday. Apparently Matt feels a lot of pressure to follow in his brother's footsteps."

"Maybe that explains why he's such a jerk," Katie said.

"Adam says Matt's really not as rude as he seems." Sharon grinned. "Of course, he told me I was a great dancer. Could be he's just a pathological liar."

"So Matt's not really rude, huh? Wish I could say the same for his horse."

"What?"

Katie looked away. "Oh, nothing. I think she may have a vice or two. Like she's big on chewing things."

"Not good. Chewing leads to biting, which leads to very painful holes in the shape of a horse mouth and a really odd scar. Good conversation starter, though." Sharon ran her fingers through 'Cape's mane.

"Horses sometimes bite each other when they're playing, though, right?" Katie asked, watching as Foxy and Jenkins gamboled.

"Sure. And they can be mouthy, especially when they're young. I used to have this angora sweater, very fuzzy with little yarn balls on it, and it was Cassidy's favorite piece of clothing. Of course, I broke her of that habit pronto."

"How?"

"Quick response. A gentle poke in her muzzle with

your finger, a really firm *quit*. *Quit* works better than *no*."

"Sounds too much like *whoa*, right?"

"There you go. Thinking like a horse again. Anyway, it's a bad vice. Horses have very strong jaws. I mean, we're talking broken bone strong—" Suddenly she stopped. There, far out on the very edge of the field, was a dapple gray filly.

"Luna! There you are."

They watched as she ran up and down the far end of the fence, near an area where a pile of tall brush had recently been cleared.

"What's that over there?" Sharon asked. "I never really noticed anything on the other side of the fence."

"It was getting too overgrown, Rose said. There's a farm over there," Katie explained. "Rose told me the owners are really sweet, an older couple. They have a few horses, some pigs, the basics."

"Luna!" Sharon called, then put her fingers to her lips and whistled.

Luna jerked up her head. She looked in Sharon's direction, tail swishing, but didn't move.

"We're still working on *come*," Sharon explained. "As a matter of fact, we're still working on *everything*. Too bad I'm not trying to teach her to ignore me. She has that down pat."

Luna returned to the fence, roaming back and forth, back and forth, like a huge gray pendulum.

"What's her problem?" Sharon asked.

"She probably sees something over there," Katie said. "One of their horses, maybe."

"I don't see any horses," Sharon said. "Do you?"

"No, but it's pretty far off."

"Luna!" Sharon tried again with an extra-long, ear-splitting whistle.

To her surprise, the filly responded, dashing over in a mad gallop. She slowed near the fence, still agitated, dancing restlessly in place.

"Hey, Luna-tic," Sharon said. "What a good girl you are, coming over here." She dismounted and climbed onto the fence, reaching over to stroke Luna's hot smooth neck. Luna looked as if she didn't quite recognize Sharon. The filly jerked her head back, eyeing Sharon apprehensively, then glanced back toward the section of the fence where she'd been before. She sniffed the air expectantly, pawed the ground twice, then galloped off.

"Definitely strange," Katie said, shaking her head.

"Well, at least she isn't moping in her stall," Sharon said grimly. "That's something. But I'm telling you, there's something going on with that filly. And I'm going to get to the bottom of it."

Nice, bouncy, even canter, good straight-on approach, find my distance, lean forward, get in position, think ahead . . .

Matt prepared to go airborne. But no. Something was wrong . . . again. He could feel Romance tensing beneath him, losing impulsion. She took off too early, flattening out as she reached for the fence, legs dangling.

"Unhh." Matt nearly lost his balance as they landed,

falling forward onto her shoulder.

"Nice form," commented Adam, who was sitting on the railing. "I liked that mouthful of mane at the end."

That did it. Matt had had enough for one day. He yanked Romance to an abrupt halt, dismounted, and kicked the vertical pole that had just embarrassed him. Unfortunately, the pole was solid and his toe was not. He winced at the pain and cursed under his breath. The pain made him even angrier. He glared at Romance. She glared back, her horizontal pupils narrowing.

"You stubborn, mule-faced, pigheaded—"

"Cow-brained," Adam offered.

"What?"

"Cow-brained. In keeping with your barnyard theme."

Matt turned his glare on Adam. "Forgive me if I fail to see the humor in this."

"Give her a break, Matt." Adam shrugged good-naturedly.

"But that's the fourth time today. We just aren't communicating. Which is to say she just isn't listening."

"Relax before you blow a valve. It's just a fence, guy. This is not a matter of life and death."

Matt brushed his hair out of his eyes, hands on his hips. Romance swished her tail nonchalantly. She enjoyed tormenting him this way. He knew she did. You could see it in her eyes.

"If you lack confidence, she's going to lack confidence," Claire commented.

Matt looked over at the fence, where Claire was standing. She had her trademark coffee mug, a horse's head with the mane forming a handle. "You need to soften your hands and relax, Matt. She's not going to approach a fence with a nice, even stride if she's thinking, *Oh, boy, this is going to really hurt*. Enough painful landings for Romance, and she's going to learn to avoid jumping at all costs."

Matt sighed. Okay, so maybe Claire was right. But she didn't know Romance the way he did.

"It's not just my riding," he said angrily, more angrily than he'd intended. "It's her brain. She's uncooperative, Claire. It's like trying to reason with a two-year-old."

"All horses are toddlers at heart," Claire agreed. "Take her around again, and then I've got to get to lunch. All I had for breakfast was a plain donut." She scowled. "Jenna McCloud scarfed the last jelly one."

Matt climbed back into the saddle. "Relax," Claire said. "Keep your center, keep your leg contact, and give her the rein she needs. But by all means *relax*."

Matt remounted and took Romance around the ring. Relax. Yeah, right. She might as well tell him to stand on his head while he jumped. Come to think of it, that would be easier. A vision popped into his head, a vision of Alec, his older brother, at a recent show, soaring over an oxer effortlessly on his horse, Sunrise. And the amazing thing, the thing that *really* was enough to make you wish you were adopted, was the way Alec had *smiled* through the whole thing. Concentrating, controlling, executing a flawless jump. And *smiling*. The nerve. The gall.

"Chicken-livered," Adam suggested as Matt circled around, but Matt was too busy thinking of Alec smiling to smile himself.

"Okay, now relax," Claire urged as he came around the ring again. "Let her move you."

Matt tried the litany again. *Nice, bouncy, even canter. RELAX. Good straight-on approach. RELAX. Find my distance, lean forward, get in position—RELAX, WOULD YOU PLEASE RELAX, YOU IDIOT?—think ahead . . .*

This time he let her take all the rein she needed. They were up, they were over. Her left rear leg knocked the top bar. Still, his landing was a little less humiliating. Not Alec-quality, by any stretch of the imagination. But a marginal improvement.

"Better, much better," Claire said, but Matt knew she was just being nice. Besides, she was hungry.

"You forgot the mane munch," Adam called.

Matt slowed to a trot and returned to the spot where Claire and Adam were waiting. "Thanks for letting me take some extra time after class, Claire," Matt said.

"Anytime." Claire gave a wave. "I'm off to the lodge. Don't worry, Matt. She's a good horse, and you're a good rider. Once you get it together, you're going to make a great pair."

"Yeah, like Laurel and Hardy," Matt muttered.

Adam laughed. "Donald and Goofy. Abbott and Costello."

"You can stop now."

"Beavis and Butthead."

Matt smiled, in spite of himself. "We gotta cool down. You waiting?"

"Sure. Maybe you'll pull some dumb stunt for my entertainment, who knows?"

Matt took her around the ring sullenly. Romance was a beautiful horse, that much was true. And in the years he'd owned her, they'd made some progress. But she was headstrong and impudent and stubborn as a mule, and if he'd known that, he would have held out for a horse like Alec's. Responsive, patient, reliable. Not unlike Alec, he thought with a smile. Well. That was a lucky match. Too bad Matt had gotten stuck with Romance, the Queen of Bad Habits.

As he and Adam were walking Romance back to the stable, they met up with the girl Matt had seen there yesterday. She was with another girl, a tall redhead with braces on her legs.

"Hey, Matt."

Matt frowned. He was still thinking about Alec. "Um, hi. Katie?"

"This is Sharon, one of my tentmates."

Matt smiled distractedly. He never quite knew what to say to girls, although they seemed to find plenty to say to him.

Sharon grinned at Adam. "How are the bruises?"

"Bruises?"

"The ones I caused by stomping on your feet all night."

"I thought that was a new dance step," Adam said.

Romance poked her muzzle at Katie's shoulder, and

Matt jerked the mare's head back firmly. You couldn't trust her around people. She'd bitten another rider last year, a young boy who was new around horses, and it had caused a whole lot of problems. Words like *lawsuit* had even gotten thrown around. His dad had actually threatened to sell Romance unless she straightened up. Fortunately, Matt had talked him out of it, with a little help from Alec.

Katie reached up to stroke Romance's nose. "No," Matt said suddenly. "Don't touch her."

"But I just—"

"Jeez, Matt, get a grip," Adam chided.

Glancing at the stunned faces around him, Matt realized too late how gruff he'd sounded. But he was lousy at apologies, and what was the point, anyway? It would be just as well if people kept a wide berth around Romance. He was having enough trouble controlling her. He certainly didn't need her biting off someone's finger in the bargain. He yanked on Romance's reins and headed into the stables.

He heard steps behind him and quickened his pace, but Adam caught up with him. "Look, Matt," he said. "Katie just wanted to pat your horse. I know you worry about Romance, but you're going to have to lighten up some."

Matt felt something burn inside, a high-power fuel of anger and something scarier, something close to the feeling you got when you were going to cry. Instead he gave Adam a wry smile.

"Let her pat some other horse," Matt said. "This one can't be trusted."

4

Melissa sat on her cot, staring at the envelope with a growing sense of doom. She was going to have to read the letter eventually. Still, there was no point in rushing the inevitable.

"Hey, Melissa. I thought you'd be at lunch already." Katie pushed open the net flap that served as the door to their tent. "I just wanted to change my shirt. Sharon's saving us a place—" She paused, her eyes dropping to the envelope Melissa was clutching. "You got a letter from Marcus?"

Without a word, her dark skin ashen, Melissa held out the envelope.

Katie read the scribbled return address. "Marcus wrote you. That's good, right?"

Melissa's lower lip began to tremble.

"That's not so good?"

"It's a Dear Jill letter," Melissa said, trying to keep her voice under control. "At least I think it is. I only got through the first two lines, then I panicked."

"Dear Jill?" Katie repeated.

"Like a Dear John letter. You know—a breakup letter."

"Are you sure?"

"It started out *Dear Melissa, This will probably be the hardest letter I ever have to write.* Does that sound promising to you?"

"Don't jump to conclusions," Katie advised. "Maybe he sprained his writing hand."

"Go ahead and read it, Katie," Melissa said sternly. "I can take it. Give it to me straight."

Katie hesitated, fingering the envelope. "We need the proper setting," she said. "It's kind of gloomy here in the tent. Let's go down to the creek."

Side by side, they made their way through a stand of pines to the spot where Silver Creek thinned to a five-foot-wide trickle. Still, the water moved noisily, like the sound of a bathtub faucet on full force, churning its way around two large granite rocks in the center.

Melissa had come here before with Katie and Sharon and Jenna, just to talk or relax. Sometimes they took the horses here during free rides in the afternoon. The last time they'd come to this spot, Melissa had told her new friends about her old friends back in Maryland, the ones she'd moved away from at the end of the school year. She'd passed around photos her friend Chelsea had sent her. She'd told stories about Marcus, and talked about how she couldn't wait to see him again.

Melissa sat down on a bed of pine needles. She folded her hands together and straightened her shoulders. "Okay. Let's hear the bad news."

"We don't have enough evidence to know it's bad news yet," Katie advised, pulling out the piece of notebook paper.

"Marcus usually sends me diskettes for my computer," Melissa pointed out. "I guess he thought the personal touch would be nice, since he's dumping me."

"You don't know that—" Katie began, but just then her eyes went wide and pained, like she'd just stepped on a tack. A poker face, she wasn't. You could tell what Katie was feeling a mile away, with her wide, expressive mouth and big brown Bambi eyes.

"Well?" Melissa said.

"Well." Katie paused. "Well, he's a lousy speller. I mean, who spells lonely *loonly*?"

"Am I dumped?"

"*Dumped* is such a strong word, Melissa. I think maybe he just needs some time to grow. Or *groow*, as he puts it."

"Did he mention who he'll be *groowing* with?" Melissa asked through gritted teeth.

"Do you know anyone named Cara?"

"Cara? Cara, with the IQ of a zucchini?" Melissa took a deep breath to calm herself. "I can't believe it. Marcus and I were like best friends all last year, Katie. We did everything together. He loved school, I loved school. He liked computers, I liked computers. He liked photography, I liked photography." She groaned. "Cara Caldwell. Cara wouldn't know an SLR from a Polaroid."

"Did Marcus like to ride, too?" Katie asked in her gentle voice.

"No, actually that's the one thing Marcus and I didn't have in common. He never did like horses all that much. He said any animal that would let you ride on its back was too stupid to spend time with. I should have known right then I was in trouble. Still . . ." Melissa reached for a handful of pine needles and watched them slip through her fingers. Her silver ID bracelet jangled on her wrist. Marcus had given it to her when she'd moved. "Still, he could be so sweet, Katie. Like when my mom and dad got divorced, he was always there for me when I was sad, you know?"

Katie nodded. "Jenna was there for me when my parents split up. It really helped. She bought me lots of ice cream."

"Marcus bought me Cracker Jack." Melissa had a thing for popcorn. Although right at this particular moment, she couldn't imagine ever eating anything again. Her insides felt sloppy and uncertain.

"I can handle this," she said firmly, more to herself than to Katie. "My mom always told me if you put your mind to it, you can do anything."

"I heard that story about how you decided you could fly to Kalamazoo by jumping off the roof."

"If I'd had a little more room to work up some speed, I would have at least made it to the end of the driveway."

Katie leaned forward. "Melissa? You sure you're okay? You seem to be taking this awfully well."

"My mom never cried when she got divorced. Why

should I cry over some jerk I was probably never going to see again anyway?"

"My mom cried all the time," Katie said. "That whole year, she was all red and puffy." She paused. "I'll bet your mom cried, too, sometimes. Maybe just not when you were around. Crying always makes you feel better."

Melissa thought. She remembered a time she'd come home from a riding lesson, feeling good, forgetting for a while about her parents splitting up. Her mom had been sitting on the couch, surrounded by tissues. She claimed she'd been watching a sad movie, a real weeper, but when Melissa had glanced at the screen, the Home Shopping Network was on.

Suddenly, out of nowhere, the tears came. Melissa started to cry, and Katie draped her arm around her. A moment later Melissa stopped.

"That's all?" Katie teased. "Not exactly a monsoon, Melissa."

"I do feel better," Melissa lied. She stood and brushed the pine needles and leaves off her riding breeches. "Thanks for reading it for me, Katie."

"What should I do with the letter?"

"Give it to me."

Katie handed her the letter. Melissa crumpled it into a little ball. She considered tossing it into the creek. It would be very satisfying, watching the busy water hustle it away. But there were the fish and turtles to consider. Instead, she stuffed the mangled letter into her jacket pocket.

"You know," Katie said gently. "There was a very

sweet P.S. at the end of his note. It said—"

"Never mind," Melissa interrupted. "It doesn't really matter, does it?"

They walked slowly back toward camp. As they neared the stable, Melissa paused near a trash can. She unlatched her ID bracelet and turned it over to read the inscription on the other side.

M & M 4-ever, it read.

"Marcus never *could* spell," she said, tossing the bracelet into the trash can. She turned to face Katie. "You know," she said with a resigned sigh, "I think that was even better than crying."

"Where's Melissa?" Jenna asked as Katie put down her lunch tray and settled in next to her at the long wooden table.

Katie grabbed a french fry off Jenna's plate. "She said she wasn't hungry. Bad news, guys. Marcus broke up with her."

"He called her?" Sharon asked, reaching for her lemonade.

"Worse. He wrote her."

"How's she taking it?" Jenna asked. "Aside from the loss of appetite?"

"It's hard to tell with Melissa. You know. She sort of keeps things to herself. She threw away his ID bracelet, if that tells you anything."

How could Marcus not like Melissa? Jenna thought, then smiled. The truth was, *she* hadn't liked Melissa much initially either. She'd thought she was too perfect, too goody-goody, too . . . well, too good a rider, if Jenna told the truth. She'd been more than a little jealous of Melissa's great riding skills, and she'd been in kind of a rotten frame of mind about losing Turbo when she'd first gotten to camp. Poor Melissa had thought Jenna didn't like her because she was black. Once they'd gotten everything straightened out, though, they'd become fast friends.

"I wish there were something we could do to cheer her up," Katie said.

"Me, too," Jenna said, trailing a fry through a pool of ketchup. "She's already been through a lot the past few months, what with her parents divorcing and moving here and all. Maybe we could do something symbolic. You know, to signify a fresh start."

"She already got rid of her ID bracelet," Sharon pointed out.

"I know!" Jenna snapped her fingers. "We could decapitate that stuffed horse Marcus gave her."

"Jenna!" Katie cried.

"Let's not resort to violence, dear," Sharon said.

"More subtle, huh?" Jenna frowned. "You're the older, wiser one, Sharon. How do you get over a breakup?"

"Jen, it's only been a few minutes. It takes a while to get over a broken heart."

Katie nodded. "It always does in the romances I read."

"How long?" Jenna asked.

"Three days, seven hours, twenty-three minutes," Sharon said, rolling her eyes. "Who knows? Give her time."

"I have a better idea," Jenna said excitedly. "A plan."

"No way." Katie held up her hands. "No plans, Jen."

"But this is brilliant. Even by my high standards."

"No plans," Katie repeated. "Your plans always have glitches."

"But this is glitchless. Guaranteed glitchless." Jenna devoured her last fry. "And do you know why? Because this plan will rely on my own brilliant skills."

"Which skills might those be?" Katie asked warily.

"My writing skills."

Katie dropped her head onto the table. "No way," she said in a muffled, weary voice. "No plans."

"Wait," Sharon said. "I want to hear this. I sense a major laugh in the making."

Jenna rubbed her hands together. "Here's the deal. We write these anonymous secret admirer letters to Melissa and she thinks some new guy is hot for her and she forgets all about Marcus."

Katie raised her head, sighed, then dropped it again.

"Okay," Sharon said cautiously. "That was the idea part. When do we get to the brilliant part?"

Jenna groaned. People had such a limited capacity for deviousness.

"What happens when she wants to meet this secret admirer?" Katie wondered.

"He's too shy for that," Jenna replied. "Shy and sensitive, yet not at all dweeblike. It's perfect for Melissa. She loves letters." She leaned back and gave Claire, who was sitting at the nearby teachers' table, a nudge. "You got a pen I could borrow?"

Claire reached into her pocket. "Here," she said. "But remember—the operative word here is *borrow*."

"Thanks." Jenna turned to Katie. "May I have your napkin? Mine's got too much ketchup on it."

"Here," Katie said, "but this is as involved as I'm getting. I've seen your plans in action, and they usually involve demerits or getting grounded for weeks at a time."

"Shy, sensitive," Jenna said thoughtfully, "but a little anal, like Melissa."

"And no nose hair or unsightly warts," Sharon added.

"Sharon," Katie protested, "don't encourage her."

"I was just trying to get into the spirit of things."

Jenna began writing carefully, trying to keep the napkin from shredding. She wrote in deep concentration for a few minutes, then read back her work silently. Very nice, she decided. Just the right touch of wistful longing.

"Let me read it," Sharon said.

Jenna clutched the napkin to her chest. "Not unless you're sworn to secrecy. Are you in on this?"

"No, I think it's insane, actually."

"Then you can't read it." Jenna dabbed her eye with the napkin, pretending to sniffle. "And it's a masterpiece of romance, if I do say so myself."

"Who better to know?" Sharon sighed. "Okay, I'm in, but on one condition. Keep my name out of it when the stuff hits the fan."

"Not me," Katie said as Jenna handed Sharon the napkin. "Personally, I think we should leave Melissa's romantic life to Melissa."

Sharon cracked a huge smile. "I don't know, Katie,

I'd reconsider, if I were you. This is pretty entertaining stuff."

"What?" Jenna demanded, incensed. "It's plenty romantic."

"If you're a horse, maybe." Sharon cleared her throat and prepared to read.

Katie clamped her hands over her ears and began to hum.

"Katie can walk and chew gum at the same time, too," Jenna said to Sharon. "We're all very proud of her."

"I can't hear you," Katie said, hands still over her ears. "I am *not* involved."

Sharon glanced over her shoulder for signs of Melissa, then began to recite from the napkin. *"Dearest little fizzy,"* she read.

"That's *filly*," Jenna corrected, while Katie hummed away. *"You* try writing on a napkin with Jell-O on it."

"Dearest little filly," Sharon began again.

Katie dropped her hands. "Filly?" she demanded. "Why would you call her a filly?"

"I thought you weren't getting involved," Jenna chided.

Katie let out a heartfelt sigh. "Someone has to keep you in control."

"Dearest little filly," Sharon continued. *"How I've admired you from afar, my love. Your flowing mane of darkest curls, your bouncy gait—"* She looked over at Jenna, mouth twitching. "Your bouncy gait?"

"It's a metaphor," Jenna protested. "Or a simile. I forget which. The point is, our shy and sensitive yet slightly anal writer is using horse stuff for descriptive purposes."

"Yeah, that much I gathered." Sharon scanned the rest of the napkin. "What did you get in English last year, Jenna?"

"An A," Jenna said. "Okay, an A-minus. But Rainford's like the hardest grader in school."

"She gave everyone an A or A-minus," Katie confided. "Even George Torkelson, who can only speak in grunts."

"Anyway, what's the matter with my letter?" Jenna demanded.

"Nothing," Sharon said, "if you're a brood mare. It's just . . . well, it could use a more subtle touch."

"Okay, you're such an expert, why don't you write one?" Jenna asked.

"Because I think this is stupid. By the way, why did you sign it *Ricardo*?"

"It sounded romantic."

"But there's no Ricardo at camp," Katie pointed out. "Melissa would know it was a fake instantly."

Jenna slapped her hand to her head. "You're right! Man, maybe I do need some help with this plan." She gave them a plaintive smile.

"No way."

"Like Katie said," Sharon agreed.

Jenna took the napkin from Sharon and folded it. "Well, then, I guess I'll have to send this." She frowned. "You think she'd mind if I sent it on a napkin? It's clean, except for the Jell-O."

"Okay, okay." Sharon sighed. "I'll help. I can't let you

make a fool of yourself alone. Just promise me this, Jenna. You'll give it a few days to see how Melissa's doing. Maybe she'll perk up on her own and won't need your, uh, literary assistance."

Katie nodded. "Sharon's right. Give it a while, then we'll help."

"Well," Jenna said reluctantly. Just then she noticed Melissa coming through the door. "If you say so." She waved to Melissa, took one last glance at the napkin, and stuffed it into her pocket.

Boy, that *was* bad writing. And it had worked like a charm, getting Katie and Sharon to agree to help. Brilliant plans were so much more fun with friends as accomplices. And this time it really *would* be brilliant. No demerits, no grounding, no unfortunate surprises.

It was absolutely, perfectly, guaranteed glitchless.

5

. . . She'd never felt this way before with anyone but Lance. What choice did she have when he looked at her with stars in his jet-black eyes and said . . .

"Boy, could I use a box of Goobers."

Katie jerked up from her book, startled by Jenna's voice. It was almost time for lights-out. She and her tentmates were in their cots reading while a windstorm picked up outside.

"Raisinets," Sharon offered.

"No way. Cracker Jack or nothing," Melissa said firmly.

Katie glanced back down at her book. Lance and Brandie had finally admitted their true feelings. She tried to imagine Lance's jet-black eyes, but every time she did, she ended up seeing Goobers. Reluctantly she closed her book and reached for her sweatshirt.

"Where are you going?" Jenna asked.

Katie pulled on her sweatpants. "Nowhere."

"Would that be the same nowhere you've been going for the past week?" Sharon asked.

"I'm just going to the bathroom."

"She likes to take the scenic route," Jenna teased.

"It's not my fault they put the bathrooms half a mile from the tents."

"Want company?" Melissa asked, yawning.

"No," Katie said quickly.

"You know what I think?" Sharon said, rolling onto her side. "I think she's having a secret rendezvous with someone. Jake, maybe? That cute guy who flirted with her when camp was just starting."

"She's a male magnet," Jenna teased.

"She's in lo-ve," Sharon sang.

I am, Katie thought to herself. *But it's with a horse.* "If you must know—" she began, then stopped herself. "If you must know, sometimes I take a little detour."

"Detour, as in stopping by Appaloosa Tent?"

"Who's in Appaloosa?" Melissa asked.

"You know—tall, dark, and grouchy."

Katie hesitated. She'd known they would start asking questions eventually. "Actually, I do take a detour sometimes," she admitted. "I stop by to say hi to the horses. And I've been . . . I've been working on this sketch a lot in the evenings. I keep a sketch pad in my locker."

Melissa frowned. "I don't know if that's such a hot idea, Katie," she said. "The powers that be don't like us visiting the stable after final barn check."

Katie felt a shiver of guilt. Melissa was right, of course, and her friends had no idea she'd really been hanging out with Romance night after night, despite Matt's warning.

"I suppose you're right, Melissa," Katie said. She grinned. "And I'd hate to get the powers that be mad at me." She yanked at the tent flap. "I'll be right back."

"No detours," Sharon called.

"No detours," Katie promised.

As she walked down the dark path, the wind sent the tops of the trees swaying in a frantic dance. A raindrop landed on Katie's cheek. In the moonless night, the arched tents huddled on either side of Silver Creek looked like huge black turtles.

She moved swiftly toward the main complex of buildings, feeling both guilty and excited. It wasn't like her to disobey rules this way—after all, she was the only person she knew who flossed religiously and refused to jaywalk. But this was different. If it meant helping out an animal, Katie was willing to break the rules. And Romance needed a friend, that much she was sure of.

Ahead, on the right, the old barn loomed. Thunder shook the sky, then silence fell, the absolute stillness that preceded a deluge. Katie glanced over her shoulder at the little white building where the stable offices were housed. All clear. Just a few more steps and she'd be with Romance. She crept along the side of the barn, her hand brushing the worn wood, which was already damp with a few early drops of rain.

A hand squeezed her shoulder. "Katie Anderson, cat burglar!"

Katie's heart ricocheted around her chest like a pinball. She spun around to see their tent adviser, Daniel, a very tall girl with cropped brown hair. She was wearing a red terry-cloth robe and matching red slippers.

"Or should I say horse burglar?" Daniel asked. Although her name was pronounced *Danielle*, Daniel liked to leave off the *le*. She claimed it saved time. Jenna claimed she was crazy.

"What are you doing out on a night like tonight?" Daniel asked. "It's almost lights-out."

"I, uh—"

Daniel frowned. "You're not up to something, you and the Thoroughbrats, are you? I thought you were finally starting to come around—" A clap of thunder cut her off in midsentence, and both girls shuddered.

"What are you doing out here, Daniel?" Katie asked, finally locating her voice.

"Oh. Stupid me. I nearly forgot to call my mom. It's her birthday. Rose said I could call from the office. How about you?"

"Me?"

"You."

"I'm just going to the girls' room," Katie said.

"But the bathrooms are over by the lodge."

"Well, the truth is, uh, the truth is, I just really like, uh . . . storms! Yeah, storms. Give me a good lightning storm and I'm in heaven."

"Really? They scare me. And it looks like this one is going to be a doozy."

"Good. The doozier the better," Katie babbled.

"You really should get back to your tent. Lights-out and all that. Besides, what if you got hit by lightning? It would really look bad on my counselor resumé."

Katie smiled, although she couldn't quite be certain if Daniel was kidding. She took her counseling duties very seriously.

"Just another minute or two, and I promise I'll go back."

"Promise?" Daniel pressed.

"Promise," Katie vowed.

"Okay, then. Say hi to the gang." Daniel turned, then paused. "Hey, how's Melissa doing? I heard about her breakup."

"She's okay, I think. You know. Under the circumstances. It's only been a few days."

"Tell her I'm here for her, if she needs a shoulder to cry on."

"I will," Katie said, trying not to smile.

She watched Daniel fade into the dark embrace of the trees. Close call, that one. If Katie kept this up long enough, someone was bound to find out what she was up to. She wondered how much trouble she would be in. They wouldn't actually expel her from camp, would they? She knew Rose could be very strict about some rules. Two weeks ago, some girls in Arabian Tent had been sent home for smoking. And she'd heard about a girl who'd treated her own horse so badly that she'd been expelled.

But this was about treating a horse *well*, Katie told herself. She eased open the big stable door and slipped inside just as rain began a frantic tap dance on the roof. Some of the horses danced in response, shifting in their stalls and stamping their hooves. The rain had startled them, sending them into a flurry of pricked ears and annoyed shuffling.

Katie slipped down the center aisle, leaving the lights off. After many nights of these clandestine visits, she knew her way to Romance's stall with her eyes closed. Romance was waiting for her hopefully. She gave a soft nicker, long and low in her throat, then tossed her head, mane tumbling between her eyes.

"I can't stay long, Romance," Katie whispered as she slipped into the warm hay-and-horse smell of the stall. "There's a storm brewing, and I nearly got caught already."

Romance sniffed Katie curiously, tickling her cheek with her muzzle. She made an attempt to munch the neck of Katie's sweatshirt. "Quit," Katie said firmly, the way Sharon had suggested. She gave Romance a gentle poke in the muzzle and the mare backed off, looking a little miffed.

"Excellent," Katie said, rubbing Romance's ears. "I believe you may actually be learning some manners." Romance had definitely improved in the short time Katie had been visiting her. She wasn't exactly your model horse citizen, but she no longer seemed like a juvenile delinquent, either. And that had to be counted as progress.

Katie wondered if Matt had noticed any change. Maybe Romance was just on her best behavior when Katie was around. Melissa had said he seemed to be having trouble with her in class. Well, it was his own fault if she didn't behave with him.

Outside, thunder suddenly ripped the sky. Romance's huge eyes glowed yellow in the searing lightning as she stepped back, squealing in fear. She slammed off the side of her stall, looking for escape.

Katie felt herself panic. She reached for the stall door, prepared to escape, then willed herself to calm down. Romance was going to hurt herself if she wasn't careful. Still, she could just as easily hurt Katie, and badly, if Katie wasn't careful.

"Shh," she soothed. "You're okay, girl. It's just a storm, just the clouds having a little disagreement."

Katie kept talking, her voice low and smooth like a calm stream, lost sometimes in the raging noise of the storm. Down the rows of stalls, other horses responded to Romance's squeal with agitated stomping and anxious whinnies.

"That's my girl, that's my good girl, you know you can trust me, we're buddies, right?"

In a brilliant burst of lightning Katie could see the fear had softened into something manageable. Romance's ears were still on alert, her whole body tense, but at least she was listening to Katie.

Katie walked over inch by inch, her feet rustling the hay beneath, her right arm outstretched. Slowly, with infinite gentleness, she reached for the frightened mare. There was a spot, right at the chin groove, that she knew Romance loved to have scratched. Katie moved her fingers in slow circles, her other hand stroking the mare's taut neck muscles. She could feel the horse begin to relax into her touch.

Suddenly, footsteps. Even as Romance relaxed, Katie tensed. She scrunched down low. Who could it be? Rose, checking on the horses? Claire or one of the other teachers? If they turned the light on, it was only a matter of time before they found her. Maybe it would just be better to confess and get it over with—

"Katie?"

"Jenna!"

"Where *are* you?"

"Down here." Katie stood back up to full height. "With Romance."

Jenna appeared before the stall door. She was soaked, her short brown hair plastered against her head like a bathing cap.

"What are you doing here?" Katie asked.

"Me? I believe I'm supposed to be asking you that question. We were worried about you."

"Well . . ." Katie rubbed her cheek against Romance's shoulder. The mare nickered softly.

"Never mind. I get the picture. You're not in love with Matt. You're in love with his horse."

"You've got to admit, she is a sweetheart."

Jenna squeezed her nightshirt tail, then went over to Turbo's stall to give him a kiss. "Well, she's no Turbo," she said with a smile, "but I know how it is. Once you get attached to a horse, it's all over."

"She needs me, Jen. She's so agitated all the time, and Matt's such a jerk."

"He really could be a good rider," Jenna pointed out. "I watch him in class with her. He's just, I don't know, tense all the time."

"Well, so is she. You should have seen her act up just now when that thunder hit."

"Katie," Jenna said seriously, "you could have been hurt. I mean *badly* hurt. And if any of the teachers ever find out about you sneaking in here, well . . . let's just say I don't want to have to be around afterward to identify the body."

"I know," Katie said reluctantly. If Jenna was scolding her, maybe things really had gotten out of hand. It was usually the other way around. "But I hate to let her down. She needs me."

Jenna sighed. "I don't know what to tell you, Katie."

Katie gave Romance one last chin scratch. "You're the one with all the brilliant plans. You're letting me down."

"Sorry," Jenna said. "Sorry to you, too, Romance."

Katie gave the mare a hug. "Be good," she warned softly. "No biting, okay?"

Together, Katie and Jenna headed down the long, dark aisle, listening to the horses shift and snort uneasily. A clap of thunder rent the sky as they ran down the path back to their tent. Behind her, Katie heard Romance's terrified squeal. Like the lightning ripping through the black clouds overhead, it nearly tore her heart in two.

"Come on, Luna. It's not like I asked you to jump the moon."

Sharon stood in the middle of the training ring, gesturing with her lunging whip, a leather-handled whip used for indicating directions. Not that Luna was interested in *taking* any directions. The reluctant filly stood several feet away, staring at Sharon reproachfully. She was wearing a lunging cavesson, a training halter fitted with rings and a reinforced, padded noseband. The cavesson was attached to the lunge line, a long lead made of nylon webbing.

And the lunge line, for what it was worth, was attached to Sharon. She held it in her left hand, gripping tightly, as frustration warred with pity. Luna was refusing to respond to any of the basics she'd already mastered: walk, whoa, reverse. At this rate it would be weeks before trot, months before canter, years, decades even, before anyone dared put a saddle on her back.

Sharon brushed the beads of sweat from her forehead. It was cool and cloudy for an August afternoon. The storm last night still lingered, leaving the sky sunless and churning. Every so often, a drumroll of thunder filled the air. Still, Sharon was hot and tired. Working with Luna could be exhausting, especially when she wasn't cooperating. They'd been out here for an hour, and although Sharon's legs ached, she hated to give up.

"How about *come*?" Katie suggested. "You said you've already had some luck with that command." She was perched on the fence with Jenna and Melissa, observing and trying to make encouraging comments. But Sharon was not feeling remotely encouraged.

"Luna, *come*," Sharon said firmly, giving a gentle pull on the lunge line.

Normally, she would reel Luna toward her now, repeating the command, then dole out lavish praise when Luna was at last standing directly in front of her. But Luna wasn't about to be reeled in like a big gray fish. She balked, she tugged, she dug in her hooves and yanked back.

Sharon yanked harder. As a battle of wills, it was no contest. Sharon was as stubborn as they came. But Luna put up a good fight before at last relenting and trudging over.

"That's the way, my deranged little filly," Sharon cooed, stroking her and making it clear that she was pleased.

"Maybe you two should take a break," Katie suggested. "You both look exhausted."

Sharon stroked Luna's silvery mane. Suddenly, for no apparent reason, Luna lurched back, letting out a whinny of protest, as if she wanted nothing to do with Sharon's affection.

Sharon sighed heavily. "Fine. Sorry I offended you." She headed toward her friends, letting out the lunge line as she went, and leaned against the fence heavily. Her legs still got tired easily, and it felt good to take the weight off them. "I'm telling you, there's something going on with that filly," she said. "She is really being weird."

Gary Stone, carrying his battered black vet bag, joined them at the fence. "How's Luna doing?" he asked.

"Same. I'm beginning to think she's possessed."

"I checked her over again this morning," Gary said, setting down his bag. "She's fine physically."

"It's the mentally part I'm not so sure about," Sharon said.

"Maybe she's homesick," Katie offered.

"We thought of that. But she'd been fine for weeks before this started," Sharon replied.

"Sometimes you see this kind of depression in horses who are bored or lonely," Gary said. "But in Luna's case, we know she's got plenty of company, and plenty to keep her occupied."

"She's listless, she won't eat, she's distracted," Sharon muttered. "If I didn't know better, I'd say she was lovesick or something."

"I know the symptoms." Melissa gave a halfhearted smile. "Oh, well, she'll get over it. It's just a matter of time. At least, that's what everybody keeps telling me." She jumped off the fence. "I'm going to go say hi to Big Red in the east paddock. Give him a pep talk about the show. Don't give up on Luna, Sharon. I'm sure she'll come around."

They watched Melissa head off glumly. "Poor Melissa," Katie said. "You think she's okay?"

"It's hard to tell," Sharon said. "A couple days ago I asked her how she was doing, and she told me she was mostly just preoccupied about doing well in the show. But you know Melissa. She kind of keeps her emotions bottled up inside."

"Uh-oh," Gary said. "This sounds like girl talk to me. Lovesick animals, I can handle. When it comes to lovesick humans, I'm out of my depth." He reached for his vet bag. "Are you girls attending the seminar day after tomorrow?"

"We're all signed up," Sharon said. As part of the optional seminars the camp offered each afternoon, Gary was going to discuss foal care. Participants would be meeting him at the farm adjacent to Silver Creek, which had invited campers to come see its newest addition, a two-month-old colt.

"Great. I'll see you then." Gary glanced over at Luna. "And don't worry about Luna. Don't forget that she's just a little kid, by equine standards. Maybe she's just going through a phase."

"The terrible twos," Sharon muttered.

"Well, anyway, I'm still worried about her," Jenna said quietly when Gary had left.

"Me, too," Sharon agreed. "Last time I went to groom her, she practically bit my head off."

Jenna frowned. "Uh, who are we talking about here?"

"Luna, of course."

"*I* meant Melissa," Jenna said with a laugh. "I don't know what to do about Luna, but I do think there's something we can do about our tentmate."

"Uh-oh. The plan." Katie leapt off the fence and checked her watch. "Suddenly I feel this desperate need to clean tack."

"I was hoping she'd forgotten," Sharon said.

"Jenna never forgets. She's like an elephant. A conniving, trouble-making, demerit-producing elephant."

Jenna wagged a finger at them. "You promised. You said to wait, and I have waited. A whole week. And now it's time for my letter-writing campaign."

"Jenna . . ." Sharon paused. "I have a bad feeling about this."

"You?" Katie said. "What about me? I've seen her plans in action."

"Come on, guys," Jenna pleaded. "I've already planned my first letter."

"Does it start *Dearest little filly*?" Sharon asked.

"Yes, but I'm open to editing."

"Are you open to psychological counseling?" Katie teased.

"What's the worst that could happen?" Jenna asked lightly.

Just then an earsplitting clap of thunder shook the air.

"There," said Sharon, staring up at the dark sky. "Does that answer your question?"

"I love cleaning tack," Katie said a few minutes later. She held up a bridle, the worn leather rubbed to a dark sheen.

"Here," Jenna said, handing her some saddle soap. "Be my guest. I'd hate to deprive you of the chance to clean a really dirty saddle."

"I don't love it that much," Katie admitted. "But I think it's my favorite part of stable chores. I mean, isn't it cozy, sitting here in the tack room with the smell of leather and hay, and outside the wind's picking up again and there's thunder rolling in the distance? No. Scratch that. My favorite part is grooming. Absolutely. Although"—she paused to hang up the bridle—"although I also like feed crew."

"Tell that to Donna and Josh. They're feeding the horses right now."

"I even like mucking out stalls," Katie mused.

"I agree with everything you said." Jenna placed the saddle she'd been cleaning on a nearby wooden rack. "Except for the mucking out part. But I figure that's a small price to pay for the chance to ride—"

A piercing scream drowned her words. "Get away! She bit me! Somebody help!"

Katie exchanged a frightened glance with Jenna. Without another word she dashed into the stable.

Romance. Katie couldn't help thinking it. *Whatever it is, please don't let Romance be involved.*

Near the end of the aisle she found Donna Hoffman, a petite ten-year-old with blond pigtails, clutching her right hand. Tears streamed down her face as she let out great, gasping sobs.

She was standing directly in front of Romance's stall.

"She bit me!" Donna cried as Josh, a thirteen-year-old whom Katie knew to be an experienced rider, tried to gently examine her hand. "I was just trying to give her some hay, and she bit me!"

Her shrill cries echoed off the old wooden walls. Romance danced from side to side, as if to deny the charge, her ears pinned back, her eyes wide . . . with fear? Or was it anger? Katie couldn't be sure.

Katie rushed to join them. "Watch it," Josh warned. "That mare is dangerous. Stay here, Donna. I'm going to go get Rose."

As Josh started toward the door, Katie stared at the dark red mark on Donna's hand. It wasn't clear whether Romance had broken the skin. It could have been much worse, Katie knew, but she didn't want to say anything to upset Donna. She was already plenty upset. Besides, Romance needed her attention right now.

Katie started toward Romance's stall. Suddenly a loud crack of thunder seemed to shake the very foundation of the barn. Donna let out a fresh wail. Romance screamed, an earsplitting squeal of pure terror. She slammed against the back wall of her stall, searching for some way to escape.

"Quiet, girl," Katie urged. "It's okay, remember?"

Her eyes landed on the door, the stall door Donna must have left unlatched, at the same moment Romance did. Before she could make a move, Romance flung herself toward it. As Romance broke free of her stall, Donna lurched back in fear. She let out a cry as she tripped and fell to the ground, inches away from the terrified mare.

"Romance!" Katie cried, but just then the mare reared up on her powerful hind legs as beneath her Donna cowered in horror.

6

"Romance!" Katie rushed toward the mare. "It's me, girl, it's okay!"

"Katie!" Josh cried, moving slowly back into the barn. "Be careful!"

"Romance," Katie pleaded, "trust me, girl."

Romance, still rearing back on her hindquarters, blinked, as if Katie's soothing voice had finally registered. She took a half step back, and Donna scrambled out of harm's way.

"It's just me, girl, the thunder won't hurt you," Katie said as Romance dropped down, preparing to bolt for the door.

"Grab her!" Donna cried.

Josh and Jenna moved closer. Romance moved back and forth in an agitated dance, snorting her disapproval.

"Here, girl," Jenna said. "Want some sugar?" She

turned to Katie. "I sure hope you've got some," she added out of the corner of her mouth.

She moved to touch the mare's shoulder and Romance took a step back warily.

"Let me," Katie said, more calmly than she felt.

"Don't," Donna whimpered. "She's crazy, that mare, I'm telling you."

"She's not crazy," Kate said. "She just doesn't like thunder, that's all. That's a good girl," Katie said, reaching up gently. "Want a chin scratch, baby? How about a chin scratch?"

Romance looked at Katie. Her tail swished frantically. Her ears twitched. She pounded a foot on the floor. But the fear in her eyes had eased.

Katie reached up and stroked the mare's soft muzzle. Suddenly, every muscle in the mare's body seemed to relax at the same time. "That's my girl," Katie whispered. "There you go. It's all over now."

"Amazing," Josh said. "How did she do that?"

"She's part horse," Jenna said proudly, winking at Katie.

Another clap of thunder split the air. Beneath Katie's fingers, Romance tensed, then relaxed.

"Let's get you back in your stall, girl," Katie said. "You've had enough excite—"

"Take your hands off my horse!"

Katie jerked her head. Matt was stalking toward her. Claire was right behind him.

"She bit me!" Donna cried to Claire, holding out her hand. Matt paused in midstride, his face a dark mask of anger, while Claire examined Donna's wound.

"I don't think she broke the skin, hon," Claire said. "But we'll take you down to the medical center in Pooleville to have you checked out. You may need a tetanus shot."

"Did you do something to her?" Matt asked accusingly. "Were you teasing her? She doesn't like to be teased, you know."

"I didn't do anything!" Donna cried. "I was just giving her some hay, and she attacked me!"

"It's true, Matt," Josh said. "I was here. Fortunately, Katie saved the day. Romance broke out of her stall, but Katie managed to subdue her." He shook his head. "It was amazing. We're talking Dr. Doolittle here. I don't know what she said, but it worked."

Matt stomped over and grabbed Romance's halter. "So?" he demanded. "How did you manage that, exactly?"

"Matt," Josh said. "Calm down. You should be grateful Katie got Romance under control when no one else could—"

"No one else," Matt said, "including me, that's what you mean, isn't it?"

"Really," Katie said, her voice wavering slightly, "Romance is a sweetheart, once you get to know . . ." She stopped in midsentence, but she knew it was too late. She could feel the hot color creeping up her neck and into her cheeks.

"Get to know her?" Matt repeated. "When exactly have you had the chance to get to know her? I told you I didn't want anyone around Romance, and now you see why, don't you?" He glared at Katie and she felt like a weak flower in the desert sun. She wasn't going to last long. She looked over at Jenna for something—words of wisdom, a hole to crawl into—but Jenna was too busy staring at Claire with something that looked, to Katie's dismay, like genuine fear. If Jenna was afraid, Katie really *was* in trouble.

"I just . . ." Katie searched for her voice. "I just visited her a few times, to . . . you know. She seemed sort of agitated and she's such a beautiful horse and you—" Her voice faded. *You don't appreciate what you have*, was what she wanted to say.

"What's going on in here?" Melissa and Sharon, leading Luna, came into the barn.

"Katie?" Melissa said. "Is everything all right?"

"No, everything is *not* all right." Claire's blue eyes bored into Katie. "You haven't been sneaking into the barn at night, have you?"

Katie nodded mutely.

"What if something had happened to you?" Claire demanded.

"She was really careful," Jenna volunteered. "And it was only a few times."

"So *that's* what all the sneaking around was about," Sharon said. "We thought she was in love. We just didn't know it was with a horse."

"The point is," Claire said seriously, "if anything *had* happened to you, Katie, no one would have known until it was too late. You knew the barn was strictly off-limits at night."

"And my mare is strictly off-limits, too," Matt said angrily. He led Romance into her stall, then returned to the group. "I'm not kidding, either. I don't want to see you anywhere near this horse, ever again."

"Don't talk that way to her," Jenna cried. "She loves that horse."

"Jenna," Katie said, her eyes swimming with tears, "it's okay. Matt's right. Romance is his. I didn't have any right." She looked over at Claire. "I'm really sorry, Claire. I promise it'll never happen again."

Claire smiled slightly. "I know it won't. You're a good kid, Katie, and I know I can trust you." She winked. "My guess is you've been hanging around those rowdy tentmates of yours too much."

Sharon put her arm around Katie's shoulders like a protective big sister. "Come on, Katie. Why don't you and your rowdy tentmates go get ready for dinner? I'll join you as soon as I get Luna settled."

Melissa and Jenna fell into step beside Katie. "He may have great hair," Melissa muttered, glaring back at Matt, "but he's definitely the jerk of the century."

Katie turned back for one last glimpse of Romance, but when she did, she met Matt's eyes, sullen and resentful, instead.

She knew she shouldn't say any more. She'd gotten herself in enough trouble already. But she couldn't help herself. "You ought to appreciate her more, Matt," Katie said softly. "She's a good horse. A really good horse."

Matt acted as if he hadn't heard. He turned away and stomped into Romance's stall. But something about the way he rested his cheek on the mare's neck for a tiny, gentle moment made Katie wonder if he hadn't really heard what she'd said.

• • •

"Now, the important thing to think about with downward transitions," Claire said the next morning to the assembled class, "is the way a riderless horse comes to a halt quickly. Picture, say"—she glanced around the class—"Big Red over there, galloping happily out in the west paddock. When he comes to a sudden halt in a few strides, what happens? He rounds his back and drops his head, which allows him to take most of the strain of stopping on his hind legs. Now, with Melissa on him, things get more complicated. Red's going to feel his weight pushed forward and he's going to take a lot more of the strain with his forehand."

Melissa felt Big Red shift beneath her. They were in the big, sawdust-smelling indoor arena today because of the rain. It felt strange not to be outside with the trees and sky as company.

She hadn't been riding Red long, but everyone agreed it was a sign of Claire's confidence in her that she was now being paired with the huge, soft-mouthed chestnut gelding. Even Jenna had confessed to being slightly jealous, although she wouldn't trade any horse in the world for Turbo.

Melissa was flattered Claire thought she could handle Red, but it made her more anxious about the camp show. She wanted to be in top form by then, and that meant she'd have to spend as much time as possible with Red, getting to know him and letting him get to know her.

"When you're preparing for a downward transition," Claire continued, "the half halt can be used to signal the horse. Keep it subtle, though, folks. Sit up, bring your shoulders back and down, and hug your legs firmly around your horse while steadying him on the reins . . ."

Melissa tried to concentrate on Claire's words, but she found herself daydreaming yet again about the Silver Creek show. She could hear Rose calling her name over the loudspeaker, she could see the spectators in the arena . . . *And now Melissa Hall on Big Red will accept her blue ribbon and take her victory gallop* . . .

She knew this was just a little show, a casual camp affair compared to some of the stuffy—and scary—competitions she'd participated in over the years. But it meant a lot to her, the idea of winning, after the way she'd started the summer here at Silver Creek. Uncertain she'd fit in. Wishing she could have attended a more elite camp. Wondering if she'd ever get over the pain of moving away from Marcus and her friends. Things had worked out better than she'd hoped—except for Marcus, of course. Taking some blues in the Silver Creek show would be a tangible sign of all that.

"Whether it's canter to trot, or trot to walk, or walk to halt," Claire was saying, "you need to keep your seat soft and your back relaxed . . ."

In her mind's eye, Melissa graciously accepted the applause of the crowd, her blue ribbon floating on the breeze. She waved to the spectators, high-fived her friends, hugged Big Red, who of course deserved a lot of the credit . . .

But something was missing. Someone, actually.

Marcus.

Marcus should have been there in her daydream. He was always there, and now . . . well, somehow he'd managed to sneak out the back door and she hadn't even noticed. She'd had this same daydream yesterday, and the day before that, and the day before . . . but Marcus had always been there in the stands, cheering her on. She'd known it was crazy to imagine him there, but it was her daydream, after all, and she'd figured she could populate it any way she chose.

But this time, in today's replay of the daydream, he'd disappeared. Vanished without a trace. And the weird thing was, while it felt wrong with him out of the picture, it wasn't exactly *awful*. It felt, well . . . not awful.

"Melissa," Jenna hissed.

Melissa glanced over her shoulder. "You called?"

Jenna moved Turbo alongside Big Red. The two horses sniffed each other curiously in a familiar hello ritual. "Actually, I called twice. Where were you? Another galaxy?"

"Daydreaming is good for the soul."

Jenna cocked her head to one side. "You okay?" she whispered.

"Yeah."

"Really okay?"

"Really yeah."

"Not thinking about . . . you know who?"

"Jenna." Melissa sighed. Her friends were trying so hard to make her feel better that they were actually starting to get on her nerves. "What did you want, anyway?"

"Check out Mr. Hothead."

In the center of the ring, Matt was making the transition from a canter to a trot.

"You're leaning back a bit, Matt," Claire called, "yanking on the reins to bring her down. Use your leg aids."

"She won't listen to me," he muttered.

"Can you blame her?" Melissa asked quietly.

"I am so mad at him," Jenna seethed. "Katie was a wreck all evening."

"Where did you guys go last night, anyway?" Melissa whispered.

"Oh." Jenna examined a nick on her saddle. "You mean while you were reading, right before lights-out?"

Melissa nodded, watching as Matt attempted to go from a trot to walk. This time was much smoother, but she had the feeling Matt and Romance weren't exactly communicating in perfect harmony.

"Oh, we just . . . Katie wanted to go back to the barn, and so we went for a walk instead, to . . . you know, talk her out of it."

"Are you babbling more than usual, or is it just me?" Melissa teased.

"Ladies!" Claire called. "Could we save the gossip session for later?"

"Sorry," Jenna said. "We were just discussing Matt's, uh, technique."

"Why don't we discuss yours instead?" Claire suggested as Matt returned to the group at a slow trot.

Melissa watched as Jenna walked Turbo to the center. He was a magnificent chestnut gelding, a real joy to watch, and he and Jenna always seemed to have fun together. Jenna's transitions were very smooth. Turbo was still a bit slow to respond, but, Melissa reminded herself, they hadn't worked together that long. Just like Melissa and Red, come to think of it.

"You'll blow them away, won't you, guy?" she whispered. She reached back to pat him, and as she did, her fingers brushed something odd, something stuck between the pad and the saddle.

A tag, maybe? Or a candy wrapper or something that she hadn't noticed when tacking up?

She yanked on the slip of paper and it came free. To her surprise, it was a piece of white paper, folded into the shape of a tiny paper bird.

Melissa held it up. Origami, wasn't that what they called it? Japanese paper folding?

She looked more closely. Pointy ears, long snout of sorts. Someone had drawn in big, expressive eyes. It wasn't a bird. It was a horse. A very strange-looking horse, all angles, as if that artist named Picasso had made him.

"Nice, Jenna, nice," Claire said as Jenna and Turbo went from a canter to trot. "Let's see that one more time."

There was writing inside. Hesitantly, Melissa opened the note, which had been folded into endless tiny creases. She hated to ruin the little paper horse, but curiosity was getting the better of her.

Dear Melissa,
  I have watched you from afar for many weeks, and

*now at last I have mustered the courage to write you.
I would have written sooner, but I am very shy, and
though my heart is full, my mouth is empty.*

"Is that a candy wrapper I spy?" whispered T. J.
Moran, a ninth-grade guy who was riding Wishful
Thinking. They sidled up alongside Big Red. "I am
starving."

Melissa looked up. "No, not candy. Although it's definitely sweet. Some might even say gooey."

T.J. frowned and turned his attention back to the
ring. Melissa returned to her reading.

*When I think of you, Melissa, I recall a very old
legend about two horses, a beautiful mare named
Aurora and a powerful stallion named Comet. They
lived on either side of the vast Silver River. That
river is now just the gentle trickle you know as Silver
Creek, but long ago it was a raging torrent, with
rapids so swift that no animal dared cross it.*

*Each day when he went to drink from its sparkling
waters, Comet would gaze longingly at Aurora and
wish he had the courage to cross the great waters
and tell her of his love.*

*I am like Comet, Melissa, and you are like Aurora.
I watch you at dinner across the lodge, across the
vast wasteland of macaroni and beanie weenie, and
long to tell you how I feel.*

Yours eternally,

Mr. X

Melissa stared down at the strange, awkward lettering. "Vast wasteland of macaroni and beanie weenie?" she whispered. She smiled, then carefully refolded the note. Unfortunately, by the time she was done, it was no longer the charming horse it had once been.

Jenna trotted over, breathless and grinning. "How'd we do?" she asked.

"Oh," Melissa said with a smile, "you did just fine."

"You coming to lunch?" Jenna asked when they'd finished settling in the horses for their afternoon break.

"You go ahead and save me a place," Melissa said. "I need to get something in my trunk."

She walked briskly back to the tent. When she got there, she went straight to her trunk and opened it. Her jacket, neatly folded like all her clothes, was lying on top. She lifted it out, sat on her cot, then reached into the pocket.

It was still there, of course. The letter from Marcus, crumpled into a tight ball. Melissa held it in her palm, staring at the ball as if it were a grenade that might explode at any minute. With a steadying breath, she slowly began to unfold it.

She scanned the page, picking out words here and there. *Hardest letter I ever . . . never thought I'd . . . wish it could be different . . .* She paused at *loonly* and smiled. Poor Marcus. Spelling was definitely not his strong point.

Melissa dropped to the bottom of the crumpled page.

It was the P.S. she wanted to see, the one Katie had mentioned.

P.S. No matter what, if even I never hear from you again, I will always be your freind. Marcus.

Melissa nodded slowly. Then she folded up the letter and placed it at the bottom of her trunk. As she closed the lid, her gaze fell on the envelope on her dresser. It was filled with rolls of film she'd been planning to have developed. They were pictures of Marcus, the last ones she'd taken before moving, along with some she'd snapped since coming to Silver Creek.

She'd get them developed, soon enough. When she was ready to look at them without feeling sad. There wasn't any rush. It was all up to her.

She headed back to the lodge, walking slowly, taking her time. The last couple of days of rain had left things changed. The ground smelled rich and damp, and even the trees seemed awake and revived. She meandered past Silver Creek, which separated the boys' tents from the girls'. It was fuller than usual, hustling along noisily. It bubbled and frothed around the two twin granite rocks that sat in its center. Brave campers regularly tried to cross from the boys' side to the girls' by using the rocks as stepping stones. Most, however, ended up soaking wet.

I will always be your freind. Just a few days ago, Melissa would have said that wasn't possible. But a few days ago, she wouldn't have thought she could spin a daydream that left Marcus standing in the wings.

7

"I'm telling you," Jenna whispered as the girls took their seats in the small Silver Creek bus the next day, "Melissa bought it."

"Quiet, you guys," Katie said. "Here she comes."

"Well, if she *did* buy it," Sharon whispered back, "which I doubt, it was because of my brilliant prose."

"Hey, it was my idea," Jenna reminded her.

"It was my paper folding," Katie added. "Not that I want any credit." Suddenly her face went pale. Sharon followed her gaze. Matt and Adam were climbing into the van. Matt met their eyes for a split second, looked as if he were about to say something, then sat down heavily in one of the front seats and stared out the window sullenly.

"If I'd known he was coming, I would have gone to the Eventing seminar instead," Jenna muttered.

"Not me," Katie said firmly, although her eyes kept darting over to Matt. "I can't wait to see this colt. If

I'm going to be a vet, I need to take every chance I can to learn."

"Do you want to be an equine vet?" Sharon asked.

"I'm not sure. I think maybe I'd like to be a zoo vet and help breed endangered species." Katie shrugged. "That is, if I can manage to get through school without blowing it."

"You're a great student, Katie," Jenna said as Kirk, one of the stablehands, climbed on board with Margaret and started the bus. "You just hate tests."

"No, tests hate me," Katie said with a resigned smile.

"Me, I want to be the first female jockey to win all three Triple Crown events," Jenna said dreamily. "That, or maybe an astronaut. It'd be so cool being weightless. How about you, Melissa?"

"I like my weight just fine, thanks," Melissa said distractedly, staring out the window.

"The category is *Future Careers*," Sharon chided, "and the final Jeopardy answer is *It's what Melissa wants to be*."

"Sorry," Melissa said. "I was just thinking about something."

Jenna nudged Sharon in the ribs so hard she winced. The girl was not exactly subtle. "Thinking about what, Melissa?" Sharon asked nonchalantly.

"Nothing. Just this letter I . . . Have any of you ever heard of the legend of Aurora and Comet?"

"Nope," Sharon said quickly. *Unless*, she added silently, *it's that bogus story your tentmates invented*.

"Who are Aurora and Comet?" Jenna asked, sounding just a little too curious.

"Oh, nobody. No biggie." Melissa smiled dreamily. Jenna smiled triumphantly. "Anyway," Melissa said, "the final Jeopardy question is *What is President?*"

"President of what?" Katie asked.

"Of Sweden," Melissa teased. "Of the U.S., of course."

"Hey, I like that idea," Sharon said as the bus started down the long, winding drive that led to the main road. "We could all go hang with you in the White House. Play Truth or Dare in the Lincoln Room."

Jenna giggled. "And short-sheet the vice president's bed."

"Wait a minute," Sharon protested, "I was thinking about running as V.P."

"What do you really want to do, Sharon?" Katie asked. "I mean, in case politics doesn't work out?"

"Actually . . ." Sharon hesitated. She didn't like to talk about her private feelings, especially something that she knew was going to make her sound hopelessly, well . . . nice. "I guess I've been thinking about maybe starting an equine therapy camp for riders like me who are . . . you know, physically challenged. Either that, or I'll go up in space with Jenna. I bet I wouldn't even need braces up there."

"A camp would be so great," Jenna said enthusiastically. "We could all help out—you know, in our spare time. In between saving species and arranging for world peace and orbiting the planet."

The bus turned out onto the busy highway that traced the edge of Silver Creek's property. "This seems crazy,"

Katie said. "We're just going to the farm next door. We could have jumped the fence on our horses and we'd already be there."

"It takes longer this way," Melissa said, "but it's safer than riding, what with the highway and all—"

For a moment, the girls fell silent. Sharon knew they were all thinking about her accident.

"Well, anyway," she said to break the awkward silence, "I like these afternoon seminars a lot. I mean, I'd rather be riding, but since the horses have to rest, this is the next best thing. I liked the one by Rose on stable management, and that talk on preventive care Gary gave the beginning of last session. But I think this will be the best."

"I've never seen a colt this young before," Katie said. "I'll bet he's so adorable. I wish we could have been here to see the foaling."

"He's already two months old," Sharon pointed out. "They grow very quickly. He's probably not quite the cuddly little guy you're imagining."

The bus turned the corner into a gravel driveway guarded by two huge oaks. *Briarwood Farm*, read the sign tacked to one of the trees. A pretty Victorian farmhouse with white gingerbread detail sat atop a hill. On the other side of the drive, a half mile down, sat the farm buildings, including a big white barn and several smaller wooden structures. Adjoining the barn was a small paddock.

"There's Gary's truck," Sharon said.

The bus parked near a pen filled with noisy, buff-colored piglets and a very large, very noisy mother.

Everyone piled out. When Matt and Adam lingered near the pigs, Katie and the others held back until they'd moved on, following Margaret and Kirk toward the barn.

The girls gathered around the pig pen, and Katie reached in to stroke the head of one of the piglets.

"Hey," Margaret called, "come on, you girls! You're missing the main attraction."

Gary and another man in jeans were waiting by the paddock fence. Katie let out a little gasp as they neared. There, in the center, were the colt and his mother. The little bay had the slender, slightly gangly look of a youngster, but his graceful conformation and alert, intelligent eyes were a perfect mirror of his mother's.

"You're right, Sharon," Katie exclaimed as they gathered at the fence. "He is bigger than I'd imagined."

"But still very much a little kid," Sharon said, laughing as he butted his mother's shoulder in a vain attempt to get her to play.

"Folks, meet Ellis Hardesty," Gary said to the group. "Owner of Sassy and her latest offspring, Searcher."

"When was Searcher born?" Sharon asked.

"June twelfth, three-fifteen in the morning," Mr. Hardesty replied. "Just a few days late."

"The gestation period for horses—that's the period from conception to delivery—is eleven months," Gary said. "Although it can vary a bit. And those first few hours and days after a foal is born are very important. Most will be on their feet and looking for milk within a half hour or so of birth. That first milk, called colostrum, is chockful of important antibodies."

Just then Searcher went off in a wild display of energy, bucking and plunging and cavorting around the paddock while Sassy watched with maternal tolerance. "He's got more get-up-and-go than three colts, that one," said Mr. Hardesty.

"Is he hard to handle?" someone asked. Sharon turned to see who it was. It was Matt, sitting on the fence at the edge of the group.

"No, we've worked with him right from the start," Mr. Hardesty said.

Gary nodded. "It's very important to have early and frequent contact with a foal, so he can learn to trust people and welcome human contact. The first few days, it's enough to stroke the foal lightly over his body, just to let him get used to the feel of your hands."

Done with his acrobatic display, Searcher ambled over to the fence, eyeing his visitors warily. Matt extended his hand and kept it still. Searcher hesitated, tossing his head. He looked back at Sassy, as if to make sure she approved of these new two-legged interlopers. Then he walked right up to Matt, nuzzling his hand.

Matt stroked the colt's head tenderly. "Man, it's hard to believe Romance was ever this small," he said in an awed voice.

"Don't look now," Sharon whispered to Katie, "but I believe Matt's body has been taken over by a sweet, sensitive alien."

"Too bad it's not permanent," Katie whispered back.

For the next hour Gary discussed the development and care of foals. After a long question and answer session, Sharon was sorry when he announced the seminar was over.

"Thanks for letting us come," Sharon said as they passed Mr. Hardesty on their way back to the bus.

"Anytime you folks want to visit, you're welcome," he said shyly. "Heck, you're neighbors." He pointed toward a fence in the distance. "We share a fence, after all—" He was interrupted by a dog's musical howl, followed by a series of piercing yelps. "Sorry about that. We've got ourselves a beagle puppy who thinks it's his mission in life to chase our cows and horses around the pastures. I've got him on a leash until we can teach him better manners."

"Well, anyway," Melissa said. "That's one cute colt you've got."

"Yep. Looks a lot like this gelding, Joker, I sold a couple weeks back. Kind of miss the guy—he was a beaut, but a real handful in the saddle. Anyway, if you didn't know better, you'd have thought Searcher was his little brother."

"Well, thanks again," Katie said. They started to leave, but suddenly Sharon froze in place, her hand locked on Katie's arm.

"What?" Katie asked nervously. "Another Matt sighting?"

"No," Sharon said. "I just had an idea. It's probably insane, but . . . Mr. Hardesty said he sold that gelding a little while ago. Which just happens to be right around the time Luna started acting up."

"Yeah. So?"

"So, what if that gelding and Luna had struck

up a friendship? You know, over the fence, sort of long-distance love? Suppose they were real buddies, and then he disappeared all of a sudden? That would explain the way she was acting out in the field."

"Sharon, that's brilliant! You are a genius. You are the equine Einstein." Suddenly Katie lost steam. "But. So what? Now what do we do about it?"

"Maybe we could get them together," Jenna suggested. "A visit to perk them up."

"Let's try," Melissa urged. "It'd be so nice to see *some* couple reunited."

"Mr. Hardesty?" Sharon called. "You know that gelding you sold? Did someone from around here buy him?"

"Right down the road a piece. Hank Parham. Nice family."

"Thanks!" Sharon said excitedly. She turned to her friends. "Now all we have to do is talk Rose into letting us go on a little road trip."

"Good luck," Melissa said.

"Hey, it's all in the name of true love," Sharon said. "How can she possibly say no?"

"No."

Rose looked from Katie to Sharon to Melissa to Jenna to Luna and shook her head adamantly. They were in the training ring that evening—the perfect time, they'd reasoned, to hit Rose with their request—especially since Jenna had convinced the cooks to whip up an especially nice blueberry pie for dinner. It just happened to be Rose's favorite, and they'd figured it was bound to put her in a receptive frame of mind.

Claire stood off to one side, arms folded over her chest. She'd officially declared herself a neutral party, although she was about ready to try anything to perk up poor Luna.

"But it makes sense, Rose," Sharon protested. "Look at the evidence."

Rose gave Luna a caress on the muzzle. Luna was unmoved. "Sure, the evidence adds up," she agreed. "But I'm not sure I see the point in loading her into a trailer to drag her over to the Parhams' just so she can see her true love and then be miserable all over again. Wouldn't it be better to just get on with your life, sweetie?" she asked Luna.

"Maybe they could still be friends," Melissa offered. "I mean, it can happen."

"Hon, these are horses. What are they going to do, exchange postcards? Call each other on the holidays?"

Katie gave Claire a plaintive look. "I don't see what it could hurt, Mom," Claire volunteered. "I mean, I promised we'd have Luna at least started on lunge training by the end of summer, and thanks to Sharon, that was starting to look possible. Now, I'm not so sure. I mean, look at Luna."

They all stared at the poor filly, her head hung low, as if it were too heavy for her to deal with. Rose pursed her lips. She ran her hand over Luna's back, deep in thought.

"This is ridiculous, you realize. No one loves these creatures more than I do, but I think we're all getting a little sentimental."

Luna raised her head just slightly and let out a low, plaintive sigh.

"Oh, fine. Appeal to my sweet inner nature." Rose threw up her hands. "Fine. One time. That's it. And don't tell anyone I had anything to do with such a cockamamie scheme." She turned to leave. "That is, of course," she added over her shoulder, "unless it works."

"Thanks, Claire," Sharon said gratefully.

"Hey, I owe you. You saved my life by helping out with Luna's training. And who knows?" She stroked Luna's ear tenderly. "Maybe it'll work."

"I've got to get her settled for the night," Sharon said. "I'll meet you guys at the tent."

"Katie?" Claire hooked a finger at her. "Could we talk a sec?"

"You're not going to yell at her some more, are you, Claire?" Jenna asked. "Because I think you used up your yell quota the other day."

Claire rolled her eyes. "Get lost, McCloud."

Katie followed Claire over to the side of the barn as her friends moved on, casting her sympathetic looks.

"Listen," Claire said. "Margaret told me you mentioned in class that you'd definitely decided to skip the show. I was wondering why."

Katie shrugged. "You know how I am. I hate tests. I always freeze up."

"This wouldn't have anything to do with what happened with Romance, would it?"

"No. I'd already pretty much decided not to enter. But . . ." Katie paused. She'd been trying very hard

not to think about the incident at the stable, carefully avoiding Matt and Romance whenever they were
anywhere near. She was in no mood to discuss it with
Claire, either.

"I wondered if maybe you were feeling uncertain
around the horses because of all the commotion. The
truth is—not that I'm condoning what happened,
because, as you know, I'm furious you put yourself
at risk—" Claire smiled. "Okay, that was the teacher
me. The other me says you're pretty darn great with the
horses, and the way you handled Romance just proves
that."

"Yeah, well." Katie sighed. She couldn't quite explain
it, but ever since Matt had chewed her out, she'd felt less
certain than ever about her instincts with horses. "The
thing is, Claire, I *thought* I was doing the right thing,
visiting Romance. Even though I knew Matt would be
angry, and even though I knew it was against the rules.
I trusted my instincts, and just ended up making Matt
furious and getting myself in lots of trouble. Maybe I
just have lousy instincts."

"You have great instincts. But everybody makes mistakes from time to time."

"I just wanted to be a friend to Romance. She needs
that, Claire, she really does."

"Maybe you should try to reach a compromise with
Matt. Talk to him."

"Talk to *Matt*? Are you kidding?" Katie leaned against
the barn, staring up at the first hint of stars. She tried to
blot out the image in her mind of Romance's delicately
tapered face and her sweet, needy eyes. "Still and all,

I feel like I've abandoned her. It's like . . ."

"Like what?"

Katie sighed. "It's like this time I went to open a lemonade stand when I was little. We had this really mean neighbor, Mr. Franz, and I went on his side of the sidewalk because it had more traffic, and he yelled at me and well . . ." She smiled at the memory. "Well, I just closed up shop. I mean, what I should have done was move the lemonade stand a few feet, right? But I sort of gave up." She shrugged. "Maybe I'm just a wimp."

"You are most definitely not a wimp. Look how you handled that dangerous horse. Not, mind you," Claire added with a wink, "that I approve."

"Was that teacher you or other you?"

"That was friend me. And since I'm in friend mode, let me give you some other advice. Try talking to Matt, now that he's cooled off. Apologize. Tell him you're sorry if you upset him, but that's he's got one heck of a great horse and you were just trying to befriend her. He's really not such a bad guy."

"I don't know . . ."

"Hey, it can't do any harm. And it might even do some good."

"I'll think about it."

"Think about the show, too, okay? It's going to be a lot of fun."

"Easy for you to say. You're a judge."

"One more thing."

"I promise. I won't ever sneak—"

"No. That's not what I was going to say." Claire smiled. "I was just going to remind you it's never too late to open another lemonade stand."

Katie smiled back. "You never tasted my lemonade."

8

Jenna peeked over her blanket, just to be sure. Yep. Melissa was definitely asleep. That snore was a dead giveaway. And people claimed *Jenna* snored. Melissa sounded like a Mack truck in the wrong gear.

She turned on her side, shielding the yellow flashlight glare with her blanket. The blank piece of paper stared back at her. She chewed her pencil, chewed, considered.

Dear Melissa,
  Again I search my heart for words

No. She erased as quietly as she could. Sharon had made her promise not to get too flowery. Still and all, Jenna was the only actual published writer in the tent, having once had a poem on horses published in the school newsletter. It started out *There once was a horse with no tail,* but that was all she could remember. Okay, so it wasn't Shakespeare. Her third-grade teacher had told her it held great promise. Of course, she'd also told Donny Clements he would grow up to be big and tall, and he was still the shortest guy in their grade.

She slapped at a mosquito and missed. Too bad Sharon and Katie were asleep. She could use a little creative input.

Dear Melissa,
  Neither sun nor rain nor sleet nor bite of deadly insect can keep me from my pen

Would that qualify as flowery? Dorky, maybe, but flowery? Not for the first time, Jenna wondered if maybe this whole idea wasn't a big mistake. But it was too late to bail out now. After all, Melissa actually seemed to be taking the bait. And if this picked up her spirits even a little bit, it would be worth the trouble.

Besides, Jenna had her reputation to consider. She'd promised Sharon and Katie a glitchless plan, and she was going to deliver.

  I try often to approach you, but your radiance blinds me like the midday sun.

Now *that* was flowery. Maybe she'd be better off continuing the Aurora and Comet fable they'd started.

  When last we checked in with Comet, he was pining from afar, running up and down the length of the

*great Silver River, looking for a way to reach Aurora,
his lady love.*

*In desperation, he galloped off to see Mariah, the
sorceress who lived in the nearby mountains.*

Not bad. This was starting to get interesting now.
Maybe she should give up on the Triple Crown and the
astronaut gig and devote herself to a career in fiction.
Still, Jenna wished her collaborators were awake.
She had no idea where this story was going. Oh, well.
It was only the next installment. She didn't have to dot
every *i* and cross every *t*, as her grandma liked to say.

*"Mariah," Comet cried (for Mariah, being a sorcer-
ess, could speak everything from Horse to Roach to
Weasel), "I am heartsick for the love of Aurora, who
lives on the other side of the great Silver River."*

*"You must tell her of your love," said Mariah
(who was also an accomplished fiction writer and
renowned jockey).*

"But how?" Comet asked desperately.

*"Tell me of your love and I shall write it down for
you," said the sorceress.*

*And so Comet spoke to Mariah of his deep love for
the beautiful Aurora, of her silky mane and intelligent eyes and proud bearing, and she wrote it all
down for him on a piece of tender birch bark, using
berry juice for ink.*

*When she read it back to Comet, his eyes filled with
tears. How could Aurora fail to be moved by such
beautiful words?*

Suddenly his tail drooped low and his eyes went wide with fear. "But Aurora cannot understand these words!" he cried (for although he was a really great guy, Comet wasn't all that quick on the uptake sometimes).

"Do not worry," said Mariah. "If you can find a way to deliver this note to your lady love, then I will cast a spell that will allow her to read it."

"How—" Comet began, but Mariah had already vanished into the mist.

Jenna read the letter back. This, this was artistry. But even artists got sleepy, and she was right on the verge of dozing off.

And now I must close, Melissa, even as I think of you in your tent on the far bank of Silver Creek, far away, like Aurora, and yet always in my dreams.
I am forever faithfully yours,
Mr. X

Jenna flicked off her flashlight and put the note under her pillow. Tomorrow she'd recruit Sharon to fix her punctuation and spelling and get Katie to fold another origami number.

Glitchless. Completely glitchless. This was definitely one of her better efforts.

The next afternoon, Katie stared at the sign-up sheet in the tack room while it stared right back at her accusingly.

Silver Creek Stables
23rd Annual End-of-Summer Show
Fun! Ribbons! Fun! Competition! Fun! Learning!
Fun! Friends!

"Fun," Katie said, as if it were a foreign word. "I just can't see it as fun. Scary, yes. Fun, no."

"You've got the whole wrong idea about competition," Melissa said as she put away a saddle pad. "But it's up to you if you don't want to. We all understand."

"You've never seen me take a test, Melissa," Katie said. "I break out in a cold sweat and get the shakes and drool comes out of the side of my mouth."

"That is not true," Jenna said, laughing. "I've never once seen you drool."

"If she's decided not to compete, don't force her," Sharon said. "I'm not competing this time."

"But you've had the experience of going to shows," Jenna said. "I just want Katie to see what fun it is. And everybody will be there. My parents are even closing the restaurant for the afternoon so they can come."

Katie picked up the pencil attached by a string to the sign-up clipboard. As she rifled through the pages, a name caught her eye and sent a shiver through her. *Matt Collier.*

She'd mulled over Claire's suggestion about apologizing to Matt, but it was too easy to imagine him laughing at her—or, worse, getting angry. For now, Katie felt certain, the best policy was to keep her distance. Even if that *did* mean she couldn't see Romance.

Besides, it had occurred to her that she probably wasn't doing Romance any favors, befriending her. After all, sooner or later camp would end, and then Romance would be right back where she started. There was no point in letting her get any more attached to Katie. And no point in letting Katie get any more attached to Romance.

"There'll be plenty of shows if you don't enter this one," Sharon said kindly.

"Yeah, but this is the one where I'm going to walk away with everything," Jenna vowed.

"In what universe?" Melissa chided. "Big Red and I are going to blow everyone else away."

"Excuse me, but while you two indulge your pathetic fantasy lives, there's a softball game waiting," Sharon pointed out.

"Not for me," Melissa said. "I'm going to the big-screen TV in the lodge to watch a tape of our jumping exercises last week."

"You watched that yesterday," Jenna said. "And the day before that, and the day before—"

"The competitive edge," Melissa said. "All great athletes watch themselves on tape to see mistakes."

"I would, but I'm a natural athlete and work on pure instinct. Besides," she added with a grin, "I never make mistakes." She nodded to Katie. "Softball, anyone?"

"As soon as I finish cleaning this last saddle, I'm going to the art studio," Katie said, pointing to her sketch pad and pencil on the floor. "It's much less sweaty. Not to mention less competitive."

She lagged behind as the others headed out the tack-room door, relieved to be freed from their conversation. Lately, it seemed like every waking hour at camp was devoted to the same topic—the show. And this was just a little show. She could just imagine how crazy everybody went before a major competition.

Katie finished cleaning the saddle and returned it to its rack, admiring her handiwork. She put away her saddle soap and sponge and reached for her sketch pad. For days, she'd been thinking about doing a pencil drawing of the barn. She liked all the nice angles, the old weathered wood, the shadows cast by the tall pines nearby. It would make a nice composition.

She flipped through her pad until she came to the last drawing. It was a half-finished portrait of Romance. She'd started it a while ago, from memory, based on her late-night visits. But something about the head was wrong. It was too angular when it should have been soft, the ears not quite right, the muzzle not quite familiar.

She reached for her pencil and erased the right ear. It need to be pricked forward, more inquisitive, more engaged. There. That was better. But now the left ear was all wrong.

Katie erased, brushed away impatiently, tried again. Nope. It still wasn't the Romance she knew.

Without thinking, she wandered slowly into the barn down the long row of stalls, her eyes still glued to her pad. Romance was in her stall. When she caught sight of Katie, she pounded her hoof and let out a welcoming nicker.

"Hey, sweetie," Katie said, feeling a rush of love.

Behind her, Katie heard quick steps. She glanced over her shoulder, suddenly anxious. It was just Mischief, the camp's resident goat mascot. He walked up to her, gave her thigh a little nudge, and she stroked his wiry head.

"Thank goodness it's just you," Katie said, but her nerves were still jangling. If Matt . . . but no. It was afternoon break, and she knew he played on the boys' softball team. And she just wanted a moment with Romance. It would be perfectly innocent, just long enough to get her sketch right. Nothing more. She'd already made her decision about Romance, and she intended to stick to it.

Katie slipped inside the stall, with Mischief on her heels. Romance nudged her with her muzzle, and Katie responded with a long, warm hug. She settled into a corner of the stall on some sweet-smelling hay. "Now stand still," she whispered, "while I capture your very essence for posterity. And then, I am outta here. I can't stay, okay, girl? Don't get the wrong idea."

Romance sauntered over and attempted to munch Katie's hair. "Quit," she said firmly, and Romance seemed to get the message. She settled down, content to sniff curiously at Mischief, allowing Katie to sketch in peace.

"I'm really sorry I haven't been by to visit," Katie said in a low voice, low enough so only Romance and Mischief could hear. She held out her sketch pad, eyes darting from the real Romance to the pencil version. "But it doesn't mean I haven't been thinking about you, girl. All the time, every minute."

Romance whuffled softly, watching with territorial concern as Mischief settled down in the hay as if he owned the place.

"Are you being good?" Katie asked as she erased an eye. "No biting, no misbehaving?" She looked up for an answer, and if she hadn't known better, she would have sworn Romance was smiling at her like a mischievous child.

The eyes. That was the problem. Romance had the most expressive, sensitive eyes, and Katie hadn't begun to do them justice. She began drawing furiously while Romance moved closer, checking out her portrait critically.

"I saw you and Matt working on the cavaletti the other day," Katie continued as she drew, talking freely now. "Not that he saw me, thank goodness. I know he can get kind of mad sometimes, but try not to take it personally." She sighed. "You're such a great horse, Romance. I wish he appreciated you more—"

Suddenly she heard something, a shifting noise. She looked up in alarm, but then a groan and sigh led her to look in Mischief's direction. He was rearranging the straw as if he'd decided to permanently reside there. Oh, well. Romance could probably use a friend. She didn't have Katie anymore, and she couldn't count on Matt, apparently.

Katie returned to her drawing again, lost in the comfortable smells, in the movement of her pencil, in the steady sound of Romance's breathing.

9

I wish he appreciated you more.

Crouching low against the stall door next to Romance's, Matt repeated Katie's words to himself and felt the anger begin to sizzle. First of all, she had no business going anywhere near Romance, not after he'd specifically warned her off. And secondly, what did she know about his feelings? He loved Romance, always had. Coming here now was proof of that, wasn't it?

They'd had another lousy class that morning—refusals, knockdowns, bad jumps. And sure, he'd gotten angry with Romance; who wouldn't, after the third knockdown of an easy low vertical?

But he'd left the softball game early, just so he could come here to the stable to make up with her. Not that he had anything to apologize for, mind you. Romance was the one with the problem. Still, he was the human and she was just the horse, and *some*body had to apologize, so it was up to him by default, since he was the only one who could talk.

At least, that's what he'd thought, until he'd noticed a sweet female voice emanating from the general direction of Romance's stall. He'd crept closer, listening carefully, and was amazed to glimpse Katie Anderson, sitting on the stall floor with a sketch pad in one hand, a goat dozing nearby, and a very calm, very contented-looking Romance munching from her hay net.

It was weird enough, seeing Katie talking away to a goat and his horse (not that he hadn't had plenty of heart-to-hearts with Romance himself). But what was really weird, like *Believe-It-or-Not* level weird, was the fact that Romance was behaving like a complete sweetheart with Katie. Calm, well mannered, contented . . . those were not words you usually associated with Romance, the Four-legged Terror of Silver Creek.

"You're being such a good girl, Romance," Katie murmured in a singsong voice.

Cautiously, Matt peered over the stall door. She was still sketching, oblivious to everything except her picture and Romance. "Why can't you always be this nice? You just need someone who understands you, huh, girl?"

Good question, Matt thought sullenly. Why *was* Romance being so good with Katie? Why had Katie been able to calm her down that day in the stable when Romance had gone wild?

"I've been thinking about the show, Romance," Katie continued.

Matt ducked back down. Strange. It was his horse,

his rented stall. He'd forbidden Katie to even be here. But somehow he felt like an interloper, eavesdropping on this private conversation. Katie seemed to belong here even more than he did.

"See, the thing is, I'm just not the competitive type," Katie was saying. "I freeze up, you know?"

Slowly Matt eased back up, so that he could just glimpse Katie and Romance over the door.

"Everybody's inviting their families, but that would just make me *more* nervous," Katie continued, chewing on her pencil. Romance snorted. "Easy for you to say," Katie replied.

"I know what you mean." Matt said the words before he knew he was going to.

Katie looked up in shock. "Matt! I know what you're thinking, but I was just . . ."

"Really," Matt said, "it's okay. Stay. I mean"—he nodded at Romance—"look at her. She's obviously glad you came to visit."

Slowly Matt slipped inside the stall and secured the door behind him. "So," he said, hands on hips, "what's your secret?"

"My . . . what?"

"Look, I didn't mean to spy on you," Matt began.

"But I'm not even supposed to be here," Katie said, her cheeks apple-red.

"I don't know." Matt ran his hand along Romance's strong neck. "Maybe you are. Maybe you are and I'm not. So, what is your secret, miracle worker? Special sugar cubes? Biofeedback? Behavior modification? No, I know. You hijacked the real Romance and this is just an amazing simulation."

"No, this is the real Romance, all right."

Katie laughed a little nervously, Matt thought. He wondered why he made her nervous. Had his outburst the other day really been that bad?

"Listen, there's something I should say," Katie said. "I'm sorry—"

"Hey, maybe we were both wrong," Matt said. *Maybe I was more wrong*, he added to himself. "Let's just forget it happened and start over, deal?"

Katie nodded. She flipped her sketch pad closed and stood, brushing hay off her knees.

"I don't suppose . . . I could take a look?"

Katie shrugged. "I guess so. After all, the subject belongs to you." She opened to a page and passed the pad to him.

It was amazing. There, staring back at him, was Romance. "It's her," he said. "It's her, exactly."

"I'm still not sure about the eyes," Katie said, gazing at the sketch critically.

"There is one thing that's unfamiliar."

"What?" Katie asked shyly. "I mean, I'm sure there's plenty wrong, I'm no Michelangelo—"

Matt pointed to the page. "See how, I don't know . . . *happy* she looks?"

Katie gazed from mare to sketch and back again. "No, that is right," she said confidently.

"With you, maybe." Matt slumped against the wall. "Around me, the only look she has in her eyes is trouble. We're like oil and water or something. I'm convinced she's planning a new and unique way to throw me during the show. Straight out of the arena into the muck pile, that sounds promising."

Katie smiled. She had a wide, sweet smile, the kind that made you want to relax and just be yourself.

Enough already, Matt, he told himself. Why was he talking like this to a virtual stranger—especially a virtual stranger he'd bawled out but good just a few days ago?

"I'm sure she'll be on her best behavior," Katie said, scratching under Romance's chin with her free hand. "Won't you, Romance?"

Romance sighed contentedly, a blissful expression on her face. Matt felt an annoying twinge of jealousy. Romance never seemed so relaxed around him.

"Sure, she seems sweet now," he said, watching the two of them. "The last show we were in, we got a second in equitation over fences. We went to accept our ribbon, and Romance looked the judge right in the eye and bit his index finger. You should have seen that guy's face."

Katie giggled. "I'm surprised they didn't disqualify you two."

"Sure, you think it's funny . . ." Matt paused. "Okay, it *is* a little funny. But I'll tell you, that day I was so mad at Romance, I almost got rid of her. It's not the only time she's gotten me into trouble that way. She bit a kid at my stable a while ago and my parents seriously considered making me get rid of her." He sighed. "That's one of the reasons we came here to this session at Silver Creek. I was hoping a fresh setting might help her learn to rein in that temper of hers."

Katie smiled again, but this time it held a secret of some kind. "What?" Matt asked.

"Oh, nothing," she said shyly. "I was just thinking that Romance isn't the only one with a temper."

"You mean me?"

"Don't tell me I'm the first one who's ever pointed that out."

"No." Matt smiled in spite of himself. "You're just the first one who's pointed it out so bluntly." He shrugged. "I know. It's true. Funny, huh? I end up with the mare with temper tantrums, my brother Alec, who's Mr. Laid-back, ends up with this gelding who's as mellow as they come. Ironic."

"Maybe not," Katie said thoughtfully. "Maybe what goes around comes around."

Matt looked away. "You mean I'm getting what I deserve?"

"I mean that maybe Romance's bad manners are related to your temper. Could be. Animals are very sensitive to their owners' moods. And take it from one of your victims—you can be pretty intimidating, Matt."

Matt crossed his arms over his chest, considering. "I don't know. I doubt there's a connection. I mean, we've been together for years, Romance and I. She's used to my moods."

"Maybe that's the problem. Could be that's why she's calmer around me."

"Well, I have to admit that anyone who can make Romance behave could probably do wonders with my manners, too."

Katie reached for the stall-door latch. "Hey, I may

be a miracle worker," she said. "But even *I* have my limits."

Matt laughed as he watched her go. Then he sat down in the spot where Katie had been, quietly wishing he could work the same magic with Romance.

Katie held on to Blooper's lead rope, watching as Jenna hung a bucket of grain inside the shiny Silver Creek horse trailer. Melissa lowered the ramp and made sure it was secure. Meanwhile, Sharon and Luna watched the proceedings from a safe distance while Sharon talked soothingly to the filly.

Claire was busying herself checking that the trailer and van were securely fastened. "Everybody ready for the great reunion to start?" Claire asked, brushing off her hands.

Gary and Margaret were standing near Katie. "I hope this works," Gary said, shaking his head. "But I have to admit I have my doubts."

"Where's your sense of romance?" Margaret chided.

"Hey, I'm romantic as the next guy," Gary said, giving his wife a kiss on the cheek, "but this *is* just a theory. I'm a doctor first, and we believe in the scientific method. Let's see the theory proven."

"Speaking of theories," Katie said, "there's something I want to run by you, Margaret. Another horse behavior theory." Ever since her encounter with Matt earlier that afternoon, Katie had been thinking about their discussion. Was it possible that there really was a connection between Matt's temper and Romance's bad behavior?

"Ask away," Margaret said, but just then Sharon signaled to Katie.

"Okay, let's load up Blooper first, Katie," Sharon instructed.

Katie led Blooper toward the ramp. Blooper was the reigning king of trailers at Silver Creek. Docile and well mannered, he actually seemed to enjoy riding in them, unlike some horses. Since Luna had only ridden in trailers a couple times and had been in an uncooperative frame of mind lately, Claire had suggested that they let her watch another horse load and unload to reassure her there was nothing to worry about.

Katie led Blooper into the trailer and let him munch on the grain Jenna had placed there as a reward for his fine effort.

"I wish it were that easy with Romance."

Katie looked out the side window, and was surprised to see Matt standing next to the trailer, peering inside—especially surprised since she'd just been thinking about him. "Matt!" she exclaimed. "I was just . . ." She felt her face begin to sizzle. "I was just going to ask Margaret about what we talked about."

"The great temper theory?"

Katie carefully eased Blooper back out of the trailer. "Nice work, guy," she said, patting him when he'd cleared the ramp. "What a pro." She turned to Luna. "See that, Luna? No sweat."

Luna snorted doubtfully. "I'm not sure she's buying it," Sharon said. She leaned close and whispered, "Matt has a lot of nerve coming around. What did he say to you?"

"I'll explain later," Katie whispered back.

Katie led Blooper out of the way, while Gary, Matt, Margaret, and Melissa lined either side of the ramp. The line of people on either side was designed to make it harder for Luna to escape off the ramp if she had second thoughts about entering the trailer. Jenna retrieved the bucket of grain and allowed Luna to sniff at it. Unfortunately, she wasn't the least bit interested.

"It would help if she had an appetite," Sharon lamented. She led Luna to the edge of the ramp, where they watched Jenna reattach the grain bucket inside the trailer. Sharon handed the lead rope to Claire, since it was hard for Sharon to negotiate the rise into the trailer.

"Okay, girl," Sharon said. "Let's go. We're going to see Joker, Luna. True love, kissy-kissy, all that mushy stuff." Sharon made kissing noises. Luna looked at her contemptuously.

"Come on, Luna," Claire said, leading her toward the ramp. "Atta girl."

To everyone's surprise, Luna clambered aboard the trailer without a fuss. She didn't look too thrilled about it, but she didn't balk, either.

"Nice work, gang," Claire said as she began to secure Luna in place.

"Well," Sharon said, "I guess this is it."

"Good luck," Gary said. "And if this works, I may just put you girls on staff as consulting equine psychologists."

"Okay, let's get this show on the road," Claire called

as she and Matt secured the back of the trailer. "Who's coming?"

"All of us," Jenna replied. "For moral support."

"Pile in, then," Claire said.

"I've just got to put Blooper in his stall," Katie said. "Give me a second—"

"I'll do it." Matt appeared at her side and took the lead rope from her hands. Katie couldn't help being surprised.

"Are you sure you want him handling *your* horse, Katie?" Jenna asked sarcastically.

"I guess I deserve that," Matt said sheepishly.

"We kind of worked that out, Jen," Katie explained.

Jenna and Melissa exchanged surprised looks. "You kind of *what*?" Jenna asked, but Melissa tugged on her arm.

"You can fill us in on all the details later," Melissa said.

"But I want to hear—" Jenna began.

"Later, Jen," Melissa said firmly. "Come on. Behave. We're going to the truck now."

Jenna frowned. "But it was just getting interesting."

Margaret laughed as Melissa dragged Jenna off. "So what was it you wanted to ask me before, Katie? Something about a theory?"

"Well, it's not a theory, exactly," Katie said, suddenly feeling self-conscious. "It's just that Matt and I were wondering if his . . . well—"

"My rotten temper," Matt volunteered cheerfully.

"You have a temper?" Margaret asked, deadpan. "I hadn't noticed."

Matt laughed. "The theory is that the reason for Romance's bad manners might have something to do with my moods. What do you think?"

"Hmm," Margaret said, tapping her finger on her chin. "I suppose it's possible, given that you've been Romance's only rider for years. Not probable, but possible."

"Of course," Gary added, "there's only one way to test your theory, Matt."

"I have this sinking feeling I know what he's talking about," Matt whispered to Katie.

"You rein in your own temper," Katie said, "and see what happens."

"Exactly," Gary said. "It's the only way."

"If Romance is reacting to your moods," Margaret said, "she'll be calmer when you're calmer."

Matt groaned. "Did my mother put you up to this?" he asked Katie. "Next thing you know, you'll be telling me we can clear every jump without a fault if I'll just clean my room on a regular basis."

Margaret laughed. "Can't hurt. Who knows? It might even help."

Claire honked the van horn. "All aboard for the Love Express!"

"I have to go," Katie said. "Thanks for taking care of Blooper."

"Good luck with the experiment," Gary said.

"Which one?" Katie asked. "The one with the horses?" She smiled at Matt. "Or the one with the human?"

10

"So what was that all about?" Melissa asked as Katie climbed into the back seat. "You and Matt worked something out? I thought you were scared to death of him."

"I am." Katie rolled her eyes. "I was." She leaned forward. "Sharon, how long is this drive? I'm not sure I can survive the inquisition back here."

"Not far," Sharon assured her from the front seat. "But far enough to get the juicy details."

Claire moved the van slowly down Silver Creek's winding driveway, the big horse trailer lumbering behind.

"So?" Sharon pressed. Poor Katie. She looked so embarrassed, but she was so much fun to tease.

Katie squirmed in her seat. "I was sketching Romance—"

"You went back to her stall, after Matt's warning?" Jenna demanded.

"Never mind that," Claire said, glancing in the rearview mirror. "How about after *my* warning?"

"It wasn't at night," Katie protested, "it was this afternoon. And anyway, I wasn't really thinking, I just sort of ended up there, and to make a long story short, Matt's not a complete ogre. The end." She crossed her arms and pressed her lips together.

"Well, thanks for pouring out your soul that way, Katie," Sharon said.

"Maybe she just wants to keep her romance a secret," Melissa said. She sighed, staring out the window. "I guess lots of people are that way."

Sharon and Jenna looked at each other. "What way?" Jenna asked casually.

"You know. Too shy to say what they're really feeling."

"I don't *have* any feelings," Katie said vehemently.

"I didn't mean you, Katie." Melissa sighed again, a secret smile on her face. "I meant . . . other people."

"Melissa . . ." Sharon said. "Is there something you want to tell us?"

"No," Melissa said, all innocence. "Not yet, anyway. Maybe someday."

"Whoa," Claire said. "Will somebody tell me what's going on back there?"

"Nothing's going on," Katie said firmly.

"Yet, anyway," Melissa said happily.

"That's the Parhams' place up ahead on the left," Claire said. "What did you tell Mr. Parham when you called him, Sharon?"

"Oh, the usual. 'Hello, my name is Sharon, I'm from Silver Creek, would you mind if I brought my lovesick horse over to hang out with your horse for an hour or two? And no, I'm really not insane.'" She laughed. "He was really pretty nice about it, too. Said he wasn't about to stand in the way of true love."

They pulled past the cedar-sided ranch house toward the pasture surrounded by a white post-and-rail fence. A rangy, black-haired man carrying a saddle nodded to them. Claire stopped the van and rolled down her window.

"You must be the folks with the broken-hearted filly," the man said, grinning. He had bright blue eyes framed by laugh lines.

"Well, we're not sure. Could be we're just deluded," Claire said. "I'm Claire Donovan and these are my fellow inmates at the asylum. Meet Sharon, Katie, Melissa, and Jenna."

"I'm the one who made the weird call," Sharon said.

"I'm Hank Parham. And that's Joker, over there by the hay rack," the man said. "Why don't you go ahead and unload your filly, and I'll bring him on over."

While they unloaded Luna, a little boy, probably seven or so, came flying out of the house to watch. "I'm Cory," he said.

Sharon nodded. "Hey, Cory."

Cory watched as they eased Luna out the trailer without any trouble. "Atta girl, Luna-tic," Sharon said encouragingly.

"Is that horse crazy?" Cory asked.

"No, just depressed, we think."

"How come you called her lunatic?"

"That's just a nick—" Sharon paused. "How old are you, anyway?"

"Seven and seven months. Which is practically eight."

"You have a pretty big vocabulary for a seven-year-old," Sharon said. She watched as Luna sniffed the air, her ears perked up just a bit. "See that?" she said to her friends. "I'll bet she caught his scent."

"You think she's in love or something?" Cory asked skeptically, stroking the filly's shoulder.

"We're not sure," Jenna explained.

Cory scowled. "No way. Horses don't fall in love."

"You sure about that?" Katie asked with a smile.

"They're way too smart."

They watched as Mr. Parham crossed the paddock, leading Joker, a sleek, elegant bay with a hint of mischief in his eyes.

"Look, Luna," Sharon said. "It's Joker." Luna gazed off in the opposite direction at a cavorting dog who had caught her interest.

"Forget the dog, Luna," Sharon said, gently guiding her head toward the paddock. "We're here to see your honey."

"Why don't you lead her into the paddock and let nature take its course?" Claire offered.

Sharon nodded. She led Luna, who followed along without much enthusiasm, to the paddock. Cory opened the gate and Sharon walked her in.

"Look, Luna," Sharon said as she released her lead rope. "Try to pretend you're excited, okay? Otherwise we're all going to look like fools."

Luna glanced up from the patch of grass she'd been sniffing. She focused on the approaching gelding, ears swiveling, nostrils dilating.

"She sees him," Katie said.

Cory leaned against the fence. "Joker doesn't want anything to do with her," he pronounced.

"They could just be buddies, couldn't they?" Jenna suggested.

"No way."

"How come?" Katie asked.

"He's a boy, she's a girl," Cory said, as if it were self-evident that boys and girls couldn't be buddies.

"Okay," Mr. Parham called. "Here goes." He released Joker and stepped back.

Joker sniffed the air, stamped his hoof for effect, then let out a whinny.

"Was that a *long-time-no-see* whinny," Jenna whispered, "or a *what-are-you-doing-in-my-territory* whinny?"

Sharon crossed her fingers. She waited for Joker and Luna to frolic to each other, to snort and chase and gallop off together into the sunset.

Joker approached Luna suspiciously, carving a wide circle, tossing his head from time to time. Luna watched him with a dull, indifferent gaze. They sniffed each other tentatively. Luna snorted, a sound of weary contempt.

Clearly insulted, Joker let out a defiant squeal and galloped off to the far side of the paddock.

"All right!" Cory cried. "Guys united!"

Sharon walked over to Luna, who was trying in vain to shake off a persistent fly. She leaned her forehead on the filly's shoulder and sighed. "So much for true love," she said. "Anybody else got any brilliant theories?"

"Told you so," Cory said triumphantly.

"I hate to admit it, but I'm beginning to think Jenna's plan is actually working," Sharon said that evening.

After dinner she and her friends had volunteered to help fold programs for the horse show. Several other campers were scattered around the lodge at the long wooden picnic tables, putting announcements about the show in envelopes or tying posters with strings to be displayed in Pooleville and Miller Falls, the two towns closest to Silver Creek.

"Glitchless," Jenna said triumphantly, taking a bite of her banana pudding. "Just as predicted."

Sharon shook her head. "At least *some*body's plan is working," she muttered. "By the way, are you going to eat all night or help us fold?"

"I'm going to ignore that remark because I know you're worried about Luna," Jenna said, taking a final spoonful. "Don't worry, Sharon. We'll figure out what's wrong with her."

"You know, I'm not so sure you're right about Melissa, Jen," Katie said doubtfully. "She's awfully smart. I mean straight-A, Honor Society smart."

"Keep your voice down," Jenna warned, waving her spoon. "She should be back any minute. And not to say I told you so, but—"

"No, Jenna's not the kind who would *ever* say, 'I told you,'" Sharon teased.

"Where'd she go, anyway?" Katie asked.

"Rose is going into town tomorrow to put up posters about the show. Melissa's got some rolls of film she wanted Rose to drop off at the drugstore to be developed."

"I wish the staff weren't making such a big production out of the show," Katie complained. "It's bad enough families are coming. Does the whole state have to come, too?"

"I think it's cool they're inviting local people," Jenna said. "Besides"—she nudged Sharon—"have you ever seen such a great program cover?" She held up a copy, displaying Katie's sketch of Blooper on the cover.

"*Art by Katie Anderson*," Jenna read proudly. "This is so cool, Katie. Your family's going to be so psyched."

"Yeah, well, I don't think they'll be coming," Katie said, concentrating on her folding. "Why bother, if I'm not going to be in the show?"

Jenna rolled her eyes to the ceiling. No matter how hard she tried to encourage her best friend, Katie could be very stubborn sometimes. "I wish you'd trust me, Katie. I was right about my Melissa plan, wasn't I?"

"I'm withholding judgment," Katie said. "Oh. That reminds me. Here's the folded note." She glanced over her shoulder, then slipped the horse-shaped note across the table.

Jenna examined it, then dropped it into her pocket. "Nice work. That paper-folding class in art really paid off. What did you think of my story?"

"I, for one, shed actual tears," Sharon said.

"Wow. That romantic, huh?"

"No, actually, I was laughing so hard I started to cry."

Jenna frowned. "Did you hear Melissa in the van this afternoon, mooning on about secret feelings and all that? And during class yesterday, I saw her checking under her saddle for a note, I'm sure of it. When she saw me watching her, she told me she thought her blanket was lumpy."

"Hmm." Sharon pursed her lips.

"What do you make of that?" Jenna asked.

"Well, I'm thinking . . . this is kind of a leap here, so bear with me . . . I'm thinking maybe her blanket was lumpy."

"Shh," Katie hissed. "She's coming."

"So," Jenna called to Melissa, "did you give Rose your film?"

"Yep." Melissa sat down next to Katie and reached for a handful of programs. "Sorry I took so long. I had to ask Claire something."

"What's on the film, anyway?" Sharon asked.

"Oh, lots of camp stuff. Like that first day, when Jenna slipped in a pile of Mischief's turds."

"I want an eight by ten of that," Sharon said.

"I want the negative destroyed," Jenna warned.

"And our overnight, that sort of thing. I took some pretty shots of the horses out in the paddock that I hope turn out well. It was around sunset, and the sky was practically on fire. And on one of the early rolls, there's some leftover stuff from back home." Melissa paused. "You know. Friends. And Marcus, of course."

Jenna looked at the others. No one spoke.

"You seem . . . better," Katie said gently. "About Marcus, I mean."

Melissa gazed at a program thoughtfully. "At first I didn't think I could handle it," she said. "But I started to realize I have other things to think about. The show. Friends." She smiled a wistful smile. "Things."

Jenna smiled in satisfaction. "Told you so," she whispered.

The phone in the tack room was for emergencies only. Gary Stone's number, along with the number for Silver Creek Memorial Hospital, was posted above the phone on an index card. Unless you were calling Gary, the hospital, or 911, it was understood you would not touch the phone, under penalty of death.

Still, there were emergencies, and then there were *emergencies*. And Claire had agreed that a boyfriend breakup qualified as a certifiable emergency.

Melissa sat down on the wooden trunk under the wall phone. Her friends would be done folding the programs soon. She'd told them that she was just going to the tent to get a sweater, which meant she didn't have a lot of time.

Above her on a row of tack hooks, bridles hung neatly. The room smelled of leather and saddle soap, a clean, warm smell that soothed Melissa as she dialed.

On the first ring, she hung up. Great. Way to look like a total dork, Mel. Maybe she should call back some other time. If she redialed right away, he would know she'd freaked out the first time.

No, she told herself firmly. This was as good a time as any. Besides, everyone was busy right now. The stable was empty, the tack room unused.

She tried again. Her index finger trembled slightly as she pushed the string of numbers on her long-distance dialing card, the one her mom had given her for emergencies. Well, according to Claire, this *was* an emergency.

He picked up on the second ring. "Speak."

Melissa opened her mouth. Air came out. Soundless air.

"Well." Long pause. "Nice talking to you—"

"Wait." Melissa surprised herself with her own voice. "Marcus, it's me."

"Lissa?" he asked softly. "I guess you got my . . ."

"Yeah, I got it, all right. By the way, last I checked, *friend* is spelled with an *ie*, not an *ei*."

"I always was lousy at spelling."

Marcus cleared his throat. Melissa cleared hers. Suddenly she'd forgotten why she'd called. This was humiliating. He was going to draw all the wrong conclusions.

"You busy?" she asked, stalling.

"Todd and I were just getting ready for a little one-on-one in the driveway."

Todd, Marcus's best friend. "Remember he's got a mean hook shot," she said. Marcus's soft laugh made her throat tighten.

"How's camp? You getting along okay with those tentmates?"

"I didn't think I would at first, but I really like them. We're good friends, really good. And the instructors are first-rate. We're having that show I told you about soon."

"You'll do great. Knock 'em dead on Black Beauty."

"Big Red."

"Yeah, that's who I meant." Long pause. "So."

Melissa fingered a bridle hanging nearby. The touch of the smooth familiar leather made her feel stronger.

"So," she said. "I called because—"

"Look, Lissa, I, uh . . . I'm really sorry. Really. I mean, I still have feelings for you and everything. Sometimes, still, I really miss you so much it hurts. It's just that you live so far away now, and I mean . . . Man, I'm really bad at this breaking-up stuff, aren't I?"

Melissa laughed, in spite of herself. "Yeah, you're pretty lame."

"Well, I'm new at it."

"Me, too," she said. "I'm not sure what the rules are. I think I'm supposed to be really furious with you, and tear up all your pictures, and listen to sappy music on the radio."

"I've got MTV on right now, but it's some heavy metal song. Does that count?"

"No. Besides, you're the break*er*. I'm the break*ee*." She relaxed her grip on the bridle and took a deep breath. Strange. It felt just the same, talking to Marcus. But how could that be, when so much had changed?

"Look, Marcus. I called because I've been thinking a lot about your letter. The thing is, I know this sounds crazy, but we had this banana pudding for dessert tonight." She hesitated. "And all I could think of was that time at lunch in the cafeteria last year, when Todd found Mrs. Lurvey's hearing aid in his banana pudding, remember?"

"He didn't just find it," Marcus said, laughing, "he nearly *swallowed* it."

"And I was thinking about the story and I wanted to laugh about it with somebody, and you were the logical somebody only I couldn't because, well, you're the breaker and I'm the breakee—"

"Yes you can. We will always be friends, Lissa. We were friends before we were boyfriend and girlfriend, and we can be friends after." He cleared his throat. "I mean, that is, if you want."

"Yeah, I want. But no more handwritten letters, okay? You need to use your computer spell-checker."

"Lissa?"

"Yeah?"

"I'm glad you called."

"Me, too."

"Good luck with Black Beauty."

"Big Red."

"Yeah, that's what I meant."

Melissa hung up the phone and smiled. Black Beauty. Marcus never had paid much attention to her riding. Maybe they weren't quite the perfect match she'd always imagined. Still, she was glad she'd called. Glad she'd taken him up on his P.S.

Good old Marcus. He couldn't spell, didn't care a thing about horses, and had lousy taste in replacement girlfriends.

Still, he knew about the hearing aid in the pudding. And that had to count for something.

11

"Temper, temper!"

Matt turned around awkwardly. Katie was leaning against a stall door halfway down, watching him try, without much success, to check Romance's feet. Each time he tried to clean her right front foot with a hoof pick, Romance tried to nip at him, and each time she tried to nip, he growled at her.

Matt set down her foot with a frustrated groan. "She's always been like this," he complained, wiping the sweat from his forehead. "How long have you been watching us?"

"Long enough to notice something," Katie said as she joined them. "You get mad at Romance, you yell at her, and then the next minute you feel so guilty about yelling that you bend over backward to be nice to her."

"Yeah, that's about right," Matt admitted self-consciously. "I guess you're saying that's not such a hot way to handle things?"

"Animals need consistency," Katie said. "I learned that training my animals at home."

"You have a lot?"

"Zillions."

"It's just me and Romance. She's all I can handle, I guess."

"I've been thinking about what we talked about with Margaret yesterday," Katie said.

"You have?" Matt couldn't help the surprise in his voice. If Katie had been thinking about their talk, that meant she'd been thinking about him, too, didn't it? Or was he just hallucinating? Why would a sweet, smart girl like her possibly be interested in someone like him, a guy with a bad temper who managed to sound like a complete idiot whenever she was anywhere nearby?

Katie ran her finger through Romance's mane. "Well, I'm not exactly an expert or anything, but it seems to me that first you need to start watching yourself to see what"—she grinned—"what ticks you off."

Matt dropped his hoof pick into his grooming bucket. "Well, for starters, my temper ticks me off. Crazy, I know. But I get mad at myself for getting mad, which makes me get even madder—you get the idea." He sighed. "This is probably hopeless. I just didn't get the calm genes in my family. Alec did. Alec, my calm, ribbon-winning older brother. Who just happens to have a calm, ribbon-winning gelding. Whereas I am in possession of Jaws here."

Katie reached for a curry comb and began to groom Romance with a gentle, circular motion. She smiled but didn't say anything.

"I know, I know," Matt said, "there's a connection. Maybe. I have to admit I'm not entirely sure I believe that theory."

"You know what they say about people looking like their pets," Katie said. "Isn't it possible they act like them, too? And vice versa?" She laughed, a shy, musical sound. "Of course, if people look like their pets, I'm in real trouble. You should see Beauty, my old muttly dog."

"I'm sure you're much prettier." Matt groaned inwardly. He'd meant it to sound like a suave compliment. Instead he'd managed to sound like a complete moron.

But Katie blushed as though she'd understood what he'd meant. "How old's Alec?" she asked.

"Sixteen."

"I've got a brother and two sisters, all older," Katie said. "All major brains. I think I may have been adopted."

"Funny. I'm convinced it's Alec who's adopted," Matt said, laughing. "Sometimes I wonder if that's why—" He caught himself. There he went again, baring his soul to this girl he hardly knew. But there was something about the way she looked at him, as if she *really* understood . . . well, he was probably crazy. No doubt she was thinking, *This guy is such a toad. Scotty, beam me out of here!*

"What were you going to say?" Katie asked, moving to Romance's other side.

Matt hesitated. "Amazing," he said in an attempt to change the subject. "She's never this calm with me when I groom her. She's always fidgeting."

"Nice try at evasive action there, but you're not getting out of it that easy."

"What?" Matt asked innocently.

"I want to know what you were just going to say about Alec."

"Nothing." Matt bent down and began rummaging through the grooming bucket.

"You guys are real competitive, is that it?"

"I'm competitive with him," Matt muttered. "It's all one-way. Which is crazy, since I'm not in any danger of outclassing him." He waited for Katie to tell him to chill out, forget about it, be his own person, find his own talents. Things he'd told himself a few hundred times already.

But instead she just stood there, rubbing her cheek against Romance's mane, eyeing him thoughtfully. "That's just how I am with my sisters and brother. Exactly." She said it in a hushed voice, as if it were a secret she'd never told anyone else.

Matt grabbed a body brush and stood. "So what do you do about it?" he asked.

"I . . ." Katie reached for a handful of silky mane. "Are you planning on braiding her for the show? Margaret said it was optional, since this is just a casual show, but it'd be fun, and if you'd like, I could help—"

"Nice try at evasive action there," Matt chided. "What were you going to say?"

"Nothing."

"Hey, I confided in you. Which, believe me, is not something I make a habit of doing. The last person I confided in was . . . well, actually the last person I confided in was a horse. Romance is a good listener, but she's very closemouthed. That is, of course, unless she's biting someone."

Katie's mouth formed a tight line. "All right. I think maybe part of the reason I don't want to enter the show is because my family would be there to watch and even though none of them rides, I know if they *did* ride, they'd be walking away with nothing but blue ribbons. There." She managed a grim smile. "Satisfied?"

"Wow. You're pretty crazy, you know that?"

Katie frowned. "Hey, you're not exactly Mr. Stability yourself, Joe Kilauea."

"Kilauea?"

"The volcano in Hawaii, you know? I was referring to your—how shall I put it—temper situation."

"So what exactly should I do about my temper situation, do you think?"

"Well, there's always deep breathing. Margaret taught us to do that when we're riding—you know, to relax in the saddle. But it works when you're off the horse, too. So the next time you feel yourself about to explode, try that."

"Okay," Matt said, feeling doubtful. "I promise to breathe. Although I've been known to do a lot of that, anyway."

"Also, I had another idea," Katie said. She had a

great smile, Matt decided. Really, majorly great. "I think we should work on reinforcing Romance's positive behaviors. You need to be more consistent with her, always rewarding her when she's done something you want."

"Reward her, huh?"

"She's a sensitive horse. It doesn't take much. A gentle pat, a soothing voice. And when you are angry with her—which you won't be, of course, because you're dealing with your temper situation—just try withholding those rewards, or a simple reprimand like *quit*. It doesn't take much. She's a real brain, Romance, aren't you?" She kissed her on the muzzle.

"Okay. I'll try. I'm not making any promises, but I'll try. And I just want to go on record as saying this is probably crazy and I'm only doing it because I'm really desperate."

"That's what Sharon said about her plan with Luna." She winced. "Of course, in her case, it *was* crazy. But I'm sure this will work. Besides, what's the worst that could happen?"

"I'll look like a fool," Matt said. "Nothing new there. Okay. My turn." Matt cocked his head at Katie. "I have some advice for your—how shall I put it?—show situation."

"Oh?" Katie said, sounding doubtful.

"Yeah. Enter it."

"No." Katie shook her head. "I already decided."

"So undecide. What's the worst that could happen?"

Katie wove her fingers in and out of Romance's mane. For a long time, she didn't speak. Matt felt a terrible lurch as he realized there might even have been tears in her huge dark eyes.

"The worst that could happen?" she repeated slowly. "I'll look like a fool." She looked over at Matt and gave a small nod. "Nothing new there."

"Is anyone going to the seminar Rose is giving on show management?" Sharon asked. She stood in the door flap of the tent, staring at her watch.

"I am," Jenna told her. She dug through her bottom drawer in frustration. "Has anyone seen my new breeches? The one pair I haven't worn yet? I was saving them for the show—"

"Four minutes and counting," Sharon said.

"I'm coming, really I am," Jenna said. "You don't think Mischief ate them, do you? He sleeps in here a lot, the sneak."

"Melissa, you coming?" Sharon asked.

"Hmmm?"

Jenna glanced over at Melissa, who was lying on her side, reading something in a secretive way. Jenna gave a subtle thumbs-up to Sharon, who grinned back. It was working, all right.

"What're you reading, Mel?" Jenna asked, trying her best to sound casual.

"What?" Melissa sat up frantically, stuffing the familiar white folded paper under her pillow. "Nothing. I mean, just an old note from a friend. Nothing."

Yep. Like a charm.

Melissa jumped off her perfectly made bed. "Isn't Rose giving a seminar on—"

"Show management," Sharon said. "Yeah, I heard that rumor somewhere. Katie? How about you?"

Katie looked up from her book. "What?"

"The *sem*inar," Jenna repeated.

"Oh. No. I'm going—"

"Let me guess," Jenna interrupted. "Matt, again. You've been with him every spare minute the last few days."

"She's in lo-ve," Sharon sang.

"I'm trying to help him with Romance."

"That's what I just said," Sharon replied.

Melissa sighed. "Isn't true love wonderful?"

"I am *not* in love. I am not even in like!" Katie cried.

"Oh, relax, Katie," Jenna said, more irritably than she'd meant. "They're just teasing. Who cares, anyway? So you're helping the guy with his horse. Big deal."

"Look, Jenna, we're going to be late. Rose'll kill us."

"Go ahead without me. I'll take my chances," Jenna said grouchily. "I need to find my breeches."

"Have fun working on Romance," Melissa said, wiggling her brows suggestively.

Jenna continued digging through her chest. In the silence that followed Melissa and Sharon's departure, the noisy drone of a bumblebee outside the window netting seemed unnaturally loud.

"Well," Katie said at last. "I guess I'll get going."

"Yeah," Jenna said. "See ya."

Katie stood, hesitating. "Did I tell you I talked to my stepmom this morning on the phone?"

"No." Jenna pawed through a nest of mismatched socks. She felt angry, and she didn't even quite know why.

"Well, they're coming. The whole family. I tried to talk them out of it. But they said they were so proud I'd decided to be in the show that they wouldn't take no for an answer."

"Why'd you change your mind, anyway?"

Katie perched on the edge of Jenna's cot. "Matt. We sort of have a lot in common with our families and competition and all. And he convinced me it would be fun, even if I make a total jerk of myself."

"*I* told you that." Jenna slammed her drawer shut, so loudly it knocked down the Polaroid of Turbo she had propped on top. "Well," she said loudly, "I guess Mischief did eat them. The case of the disappearing breeches. At least I can take solace in the fact that he'll have indigestion for weeks."

Katie reached under the mattress and felt around for a moment. "These look familiar?" she asked, holding up a pair of new tan riding breeches.

"How did you—" Jenna gasped. "And to think I was ready to suggest the cooks add goat burger to the menu."

"Elementary, my dear McCloud," Katie said. "You put your shirts under your mattress at home so you won't have to iron them. Simple logic. Plus, I *am* your best friend."

Jenna folded the breeches, avoiding her friend's gaze. "Are you still?"

"Jenna!" Katie cried in exasperation. "What do you—

wait a minute. Is this about Matt? Because I've been spending so much time with him?"

"All your time with him," Jenna reminded her. "On the cross-country ride yesterday, you barely even spoke to Melissa and Sharon and me. And yesterday afternoon when we were helping Claire set up the jump course, you two were walking around like someone had welded you together." She sighed and plopped down on the cot. "Look, I just don't want you to turn into one of the girls who becomes totally guy-obsessed and forgets about her friends. You know. Like Lydia Crandall?"

"I am not Lydia Crandall," Katie said. "I'm me. You'll always be my best friend in the whole world, Jenna. Forever. I mean, Matt's nice. But he's still a guy. There are some things I just can't talk to him about."

Jenna smiled. She felt better, hearing Katie say it. Until this minute, she hadn't realized how left out she'd been feeling.

"But you have to promise me the same thing," Katie said firmly. "That you won't weird out on me when you start liking some guy."

"I promise that I will never let some imaginary guy get in the way of our real friendship."

"That's better," Katie said. "Hey, speaking of imaginary guys, what are you going to do about Melissa?"

Jenna shrugged. "Just keep going, I guess. I mean, she does seem happier, don't you think?"

"Yeah, but I'm not sure if the notes are the reason. Could be she's getting over Marcus on her own. Or maybe she's just excited about the show."

Jenna frowned. "I guess I didn't think about how to end all this. I mean, Mr. X can't exactly stop writing her, can he? That would be two breakups in a month. She'd be devastated. Even if he doesn't really exist."

"What about when camp ends?" Katie wondered.

"Then Mr. X will go back to his hometown of . . . of X-ville, and Melissa will remember him fondly as a summer romance."

"But what if she starts asking questions?"

"She won't," Jenna said.

"But what if she does?"

"As they say here at Silver Creek, we'll jump that fence when we come to it."

12

When Katie was done with her lesson the next morning, she wandered over to one of the training rings, where she found Matt cantering with Romance. When he saw Katie, his face lit up and he waved.

"How's he doing?" Katie asked Claire, who was watching him from her position near the gate.

Claire smiled. "Not bad. I think you and your temper lessons are beginning to have an effect. But he's still tense, and that has to affect Romance. I told him he could have a few extra minutes after class to work on his jumps."

"Breathe!" Katie called.

Matt nodded. "Easy for you to say."

"What's that you're holding?" Katie asked Claire, pointing to the stack of white cards in her hand.

"Score cards for judging the show. Nothing formal. This isn't exactly an AHSA show."

Katie felt a little shiver go through her. "May I see?"

"Well—" Claire hesitated. "Okay. But don't let them freak you out, okay?"

Katie scanned the list anxiously. *Inclusion of maneuvers not specified. Rider forgets pattern. Starting circles out of lead. Posting on wrong diagonal. Break of gait. Fall to the ground by horse or rider—*

"Here." She shoved the cards back at Claire.

"Relax, Katie," Claire said. "Even with your vivid imagination, you can't actually see yourself committing all those sins, can you?"

"Easily." Katie turned her attention back to Matt, who'd made a rough transition to canter and was making his approach to the low vertical in the center of the ring.

"I'm really glad you changed your mind about the show. It'll be fun. You'll see."

"That's what they told me the first time I went to the dentist."

"I'll be over by that oak tree, if Matt has any questions."

Katie nodded. Matt was way too tense, Claire was right. It was like watching a tin soldier ride a real flesh-and-blood horse. "Breathe!" she called again.

His approach was slow, his hands rough, and Romance made an undignified attempt to run out at the last second. Fortunately, he kept her on course. But it was no wonder, with his unbalanced seat, that she wasn't much interested in Matt's idea of fun.

Matt knew it had been a bad jump. Katie could see

it in his face. He rode over to her and stopped. "I'm telling you, it's her," he muttered, his mouth in a tight line. "If she'd just listen . . ." His voice rose in anger.

"Hey, Kilauea," Katie chided.

"It's not funny, Katie," Matt growled. "The show's day after tomorrow, and if we don't get our act together—"

"What? What's the worst that could happen?" Katie asked.

Matt pursed his lips. "I could totally blow it," he said darkly. "I could—"

"Look like a fool?" Katie supplied.

Matt hesitated. She could see the hint of a smile surfacing. "No, I could look like a *total* fool." He rolled his eyes. "Sorry. Old habits die hard. *You* try to reform your personality overnight. On second thought," he added with a grin, "don't. I like you just the way you are."

Katie felt the beginnings of a blush. She reached over to pat Romance's hot neck. "Hey, did you praise her when she finally took the jump?"

"No, it was so lousy—" Matt sighed. "Oops. This is harder than it looks. It's too late now, though."

"It's never too late," Katie said.

Matt reached down and gave Romance a long pat. "Sorry, girl. It's me, not you. I see the error of my ways. Thanks to your friend Katie here."

He squared his shoulders. "Well, here goes nothing."

"Try to relax," Katie suggested. "I don't know much about jumping, but you look tense, and that means you feel tense to Romance. Don't forget to breathe."

Matt sighed. "Breathe, she says. You remind me of this choir teacher I had in grade school. Ms. Hyland. 'Breathe with your diaphragm, children!' " He imitated a squeaky woman's voice. "Trouble was, none of us knew where our diaphragms were, and she never bothered to tell us. I was pretty much convinced it was located somewhere on the bottom of my foot."

Katie laughed as Matt and Romance took off around the ring again. Suddenly she had an idea. "Matt!" she cried.

"Yeah?" he called from the far side of the ring.

"Do you know the words to 'The Star-Spangled Banner'?"

She could see the muscles in Matt's neck tense up. He slowed Romance to a walk. "Katie. I'm kind of having enough trouble concentrating here."

"Maybe that's your problem," Katie said. "Just try singing the national anthem while you jump, okay?"

"I have a better idea. Why don't I do a handstand while I recite the Gettysburg Address?"

"Just try it."

Matt continued around the ring. She couldn't be sure, but he seemed to be muttering something under his breath. But when he passed by at a collected canter, she heard him. " . . . What so proudly we hailed . . ."

He approached the jump, still singing, his body in much better position. He found his distance and Romance took off in a smooth, nearly flawless jump. When they landed, Katie could still hear Matt singing. " . . . the ramparts we watched, were so . . ."

He rode over to her, patting Romance as he went. "I can't believe it. It worked."

"I figured if you were singing, you'd *have* to be breathing nice and evenly," Katie said.

"Katie Anderson, you are pretty amazing." Matt shook his head. "Now, one more thing."

"What's that?"

"Does it have to be 'The Star-Spangled Banner'? Because those high notes are really killers."

Katie waved good-bye to Matt and headed back to the tent slowly, listening to the birds gossiping in the trees she passed. She thought about the show and felt a wave of panic.

Then she thought of Matt.

She wondered what if they were having leftover goulash surprise for dinner. She hated goulash surprise.

Then she thought of Matt.

She tried to decide if she had time to go over to the art studio and finish up the sketch she'd been working on.

Then she thought of Matt.

Was this what liking a guy was all about? Your brain veering off in wild directions, like a bike without handlebars? And were your palms always sweaty? Would she have to go around with sweaty palms permanently? Did everyone have sweaty palms? Her mom? Sharon?

No. Sharon was way too cool to have sweaty palms.

How could she ever hold hands with a guy if her palms were always sweating? Was there some kind of treatment for palm problems?

No. She would have seen it advertised in one of her teen magazines.

It was obvious that her sweaty palms were freaks of nature. There was only one solution. She could never, ever hold hands with Matt.

Not unless she had mittens on.

Matt walked Romance around the ring to cool her down, enjoying the sunlight on his back and the rush of accomplishment from their good workout. Still, a workout was one thing, the show was quite another. The thought of competing made him grit his teeth.

Then he thought of Katie.

He wondered if they were going to have leftover goulash surprise for dinner. He loved goulash surprise, especially on the second day.

Then he thought of Katie.

He wondered if he'd have time after grooming Romance for a little b-ball with the guys.

Then he thought of Katie.

Was this what liking a girl was all about? Your brain veering off in wild directions, like a car without a driver? And were your palms always sweaty? Was this a permanent condition, like eye color? Did Adam's palms sweat when he talked to girls?

No. Adam was way too cool to sweat, unless he was playing football.

Was there some kind of professional he could consult about his sweaty palms? A hand specialist? Was there a cure for his disorder?

It was obvious that Matt was completely, utterly

not cool. He could never hold hands with Katie. Never.
Not unless he was wearing gloves.

This time, the note was pinned to her locker. Another origami horse, although this one seemed to have rather droopy ears. Melissa smiled. With all the preparations for the show tomorrow, she was surprised Mr. X had found the time.

Melissa sat down on a storage trunk and carefully unfolded the note. *Dear Melissa*, read the familiar messy handwriting.

Again I write you of the tender legend of Comet and Aurora. When last we saw Comet, he had his declaration of love, written by the old sorceress, Mariah. He took the love letter to the bank of the great Silver River, filled with hope. There on the other side of the dark dangerous water, prancing gaily, was Aurora, her beautiful black mane flowing in the breeze like the great river itself.

Comet folded up the note into a sort of paper bird (the legend's not really clear on how this was accomplished, what with him lacking fingers, but then, that's how legends are).

Melissa paused to giggle. She looked up, careful to make sure no one had seen her, then continued reading.

Comet took his love letter in his mouth and threw back his head, launching the note into the air. Well,

*naturally, it didn't go far, since there was a brisk
wind coming out of the northwest and Comet wasn't
exactly an aerospace engineer. It landed at his feet,
in fact, far from its destination.*

*Comet hung his head, watching the rushing waters
he dared not cross. You can imagine how bummed
he was.*

*Soon a swift-moving fish floated to the surface, a
shimmering rainbow-colored trout. "Why so bummed,
big horse?" he asked.*

*"I cannot get this letter to the other side," Comet
explained.*

"What's in it?" asked the fish.

*"All my feelings for the beautiful Aurora," said Com-
et. "But I cannot brave the current."*

"I will take the letter for you," said the fish.

*Gratefully, Comet presented the note to the trout,
who took it in his mouth and slipped deep into the
powerful current.*

*Comet waited anxiously, prancing back and forth on
the bank, watching for the moment when the trout
would reappear on the other side and give Aurora
the note.*

*Suddenly he heard a splash at his feet. It was the
trout, gasping and weary. He dropped the note on
the bank.*

"But why didn't you deliver it?" Comet asked.

*"It was too heavy," the trout complained. "Perhaps
you have too many feelings."*

Poor Comet. You can see, Melissa, why I sympa-

thize with him. For I have so much to say, and so little time. Soon camp will be over, and then what? I shall have to exist on my memories alone, my memories of your dark mysterious eyes and sweet smile.

I remain forever yours,
Mr. X

Melissa put down the note. "Exist on memories alone?" she said under her breath. "What fun would there be in that, Mr. X?"

She searched around for a piece of paper and a pen, at last locating them in a cabinet. For a moment she paused. This had to be good. Compelling. Convincing. As moving as the notes she'd been receiving.

Dear Mr. X,
Your letters have moved me beyond mere words. I cannot leave camp without meeting you, just once, to sustain me through the long dark hours of the school year I will soon have to face without you.

Meet me tomorrow in the tack room after the final show event. Don't let me down, Mr. X. My heart has been broken once, but now you've mended it. Were it to break again, not all the superglue on the planet could put it back together.

Hopefully,
Melissa.
P.S. Can't wait to hear what happens to Comet and Aurora.

Melissa folded up the note and wrote *Mr. X* on the cover. She pinned it on the bulletin board by the lockers where she knew it would be seen. Then she smiled a secret smile and slipped out the door.

13

"Luna, girl, why won't you tell me what's bothering you?" Sharon asked early that evening as they stood in one of the training rings together.

All around them, campers buzzed about in high gear, working on last-minute preparations for the show tomorrow. In the main arena, a group of teachers was checking the measurements between jumps to be sure they were perfectly aligned. A few die-hard perfectionists were working on technique while counselors or teachers offered encouragement or advice. In Rose's office, Margaret had an iron and ironing board set up so riders could make sure their clothes would look perfect for the big day. She'd made it very clear, however, that ironing was the responsibility of the campers.

It wasn't the high-intensity excitement of some of the shows Sharon had been in with Cassidy, back in the old days. But this one had an air of fun about it. It was like a practice drill, a chance for all the campers to

show their stuff without too much pressure. Not that
you'd know that, judging from her three tentmates.
Melissa and Jenna were both rushing around madly,
while Katie seemed more anxious than excited.

Sharon sighed wistfully as she adjusted the cavesson Luna was wearing. She knew she wasn't ready to
compete yet, not when her legs were still so weak, but
she had to admit she missed the rush of competing.
At least she had Luna to distract her, although all the
filly seemed to want to do was stare mournfully out at
the distant pasture, lost in her own private reverie.

"I wish I could crawl into that head of yours for a
minute," Sharon said, shooing away a fly that was
tormenting Luna's right ear.

"Sharon!" Jenna came rushing toward the fence in
her usual high gear. She was clutching a piece of paper
in her right hand. "Where's Melissa?"

"She went to give Big Red a pep talk."

"How about Katie?"

"She went to give Matt a pep talk. Or maybe it was
the other way around. You want me to give you a pep
talk? You look like you could use one."

"We have a problem," Jenna said, clambering over
the fence.

"I'm not sure I like that plural pronoun."

Jenna held out her palm. "I found this note by the
lockers. Look who it's for!"

"Mr. *X*?" Sharon took a step back. "Now I *know* I
don't like that pronoun."

"Melissa wants to meet him. Me. Us. Can you believe
it?" Jenna cried. She paced back and forth while Luna

watched her sullenly. "What are we going to do?"

"It's a good thing I'm not the kind of person who'd say *I told you so*, because this situation really cries out for some gloating." Sharon reached for the letter and scanned it. "Whoa." She passed it back to Jenna, who stuffed it into her pocket. "You *are* in trouble."

"You mean *we*."

"Actually, *you* was the word I had in mind."

Jenna rubbed her forehead. "If we tell Melissa the truth, she'll feel terrible. But if Mr. X doesn't show up—"

"You mean you."

"I *mean* we. If Mr. X doesn't show up—"

"Which would be difficult," Sharon pointed out, "what with him being a figment of your warped imagination."

"I was just trying to help," Jenna whined. "And now I've created a monster."

"Actually, to be perfectly accurate, you've created a really corny invisible dweeb."

"Sharon," Jenna said, hands on hips. "You're in this, too. You're the one who came up with the whole legend idea. Which, incidentally, since we're being critical here, has no ending."

"You know, you may be a lot shorter than I am, but when you get all feisty like this, you almost—"

"Scare you?" Jenna supplied.

"No, you remind me of this Yorkshire terrier I had as a kid. Real yappy. Every time my mom came home from work she'd wet the carpet."

Jenna managed a grin. "The dog or your mom?"

Just then Katie emerged from the stable, carrying a white package in her hand. "How's Luna doing?" she called as she approached.

"She's not," Sharon said. "Hey, that's not another letter, is it?"

"This?" Katie opened the gate and joined them. "No, these are Melissa's photos. Rose picked them up today. Melissa asked me to take them back to the tent. She's still with Red." She gave Luna a hug. "What do you mean, *another*?"

Jenna stuck out the note. "Read," she said wearily. "From Melissa."

"She wants to meet Mr. X," Sharon said.

"Oh, no."

"Go ahead," Jenna said, leaning against the fence, a resigned expression on her face. "Say I told you so and get it over with."

"I'm not that kind of person, Jen," Katie said, glancing over the letter.

"Fortunately, I am," Sharon said.

Katie folded up the note. "Maybe you could just pretend you never got the note."

"I can't do that. She'll think Mr. X is ignoring her. No matter what we do, one way or another we're going to end up hurting Melissa's feelings."

"There you go with that pesky pronoun problem," Sharon said.

"I knew this would happen," Katie said, sighing.

"Is that anything like I told you so?" Sharon inquired.

"Okay, okay," Jenna said. "But I had the best of intentions. I just wanted to make her feel better, and now we're going to end up making her feel a thousand times worse." Jenna kicked at a tuft of grass by the fence. "Talk about bad timing. Couldn't she have written Mr. X after the show? How am I supposed to concentrate on my riding with this hanging over my head?"

"That's not your main problem," Katie said.

"I know, I know. My main problem is I don't want to hurt Melissa's feelings. Hey. How about if I leave her another note and tell her I'm horribly disfigured like the Hunchback of Notre Dame and can't bear to meet her? You know, the whole Beauty and the Beast thing."

"Jenna, Mr. X obviously attends camp," Sharon said. "It's not that big a place. Don't you think she would have noticed the Hunchback of Notre Dame getting a chili dog in the lunch line?"

"I'm horse doodoo," Jenna said. "Finished. Kaput. She'll hate me."

"Hey, speaking of doodoo," Katie said with a grin, "check out this picture Melissa took of you. Remember the first day we met, when you slipped on some of Mischief's . . . uh, you know."

Katie opened the envelope and flipped through several photos. She handed one to Jenna. Sharon moved closer so she could get a look. There was Jenna, flat on her behind, looking furious and mortified at the same time.

"Oh, this picture has serious blackmail potential," Sharon remarked gleefully.

"I want that burned," Jenna threatened.

"Nope." Katie shook her head. "After tomorrow, Melissa may need to use it for target practice."

For the next few minutes, the girls thumbed through Melissa's photos. She had a nice eye, Sharon thought, and had managed to capture all the best moments of their summer together. Their first few awkward days in the tent. Their overnight trip. Lessons. A breakfast food fight in the lodge. Late-night campfires. And lots of smiles . . . goofy, wistful, sincere.

Sharon reached for a photo Melissa had taken of the four of them near the west paddock a few weeks back. She'd put the camera on automatic timer and set it in the crook of a nearby tree branch. There they stood, leaning against the fence—Katie, smiling sincerely; Melissa, preoccupied and a little stern; Jenna, mugging. And Sharon was looking over her shoulder, her face only half-visible.

At Luna, that's what she'd been looking at. You could just make out the silver-gray blur as she galloped along that same stretch of fence that separated Silver Creek's property from Mr. Hardesty's.

Her mane was floating in the air, her steps were high. She looked happy.

Sharon held up the photo for Luna to see. "Look. See? That's you, Luna. Frisky. Galloping. Happy. Troublesome. Remember this Luna? Remember her?"

As Sharon handed the picture to Katie, something caught her eye. A brownish blur near the other side of the fence, smaller than Luna, much smaller.

"What is that?" Sharon asked Jenna, pointing to the image.

"A ghost, I'm guessing."

Katie peered at it. "A dog, I'll bet."

"Maybe a ghost dog," Jenna volunteered.

Sharon squinted at the image. "A ghost dog," she repeated.

"Sharon, what are you thinking?" Katie asked.

"Me? Nothing," Sharon said quickly. "Nothing at all." She was done with theories. Absolutely done.

Then she looked into Luna's lost, wistful eyes and instantly changed her mind.

"Attention, riders!" Rose's voice boomed across the grounds over the loudspeaker. "The first class in the Silver Creek Stables Twenty-third Annual Summer Camp Horse Show will commence in fifteen minutes. All entrants in the lead-line class should be ready in the warm-up ring in ten minutes with their handlers." Rose paused. "That's ten minutes, gang. Not eleven. Not eleven and a half. Oh. By the way, has anyone seen Nikki Baumgartner's lucky horseshoe pin? She's worried Mischief may have eaten it for breakfast."

Sharon laughed as she clipped Blooper to the cross-ties near his stall. "I can see this show's going to be a little more casual than the Classic."

Katie reached for the curry comb in her grooming bucket. "Casual? You call this"—she gestured at the frantic riders rushing to and fro—"casual? I've seen two people crying already, and the show hasn't even started!"

Sharon glanced down the aisle to the spot where Matt had Romance cross-tied. He was cleaning a brush with a curry comb, using brisk, agitated strokes. "I don't suppose one of them was Matt?" Sharon teased in a whisper.

"He's hardly spoken a word, he's so uptight. I'm worried it's going to affect Romance. She's so sensitive to his moods."

"Well, Blooper here seems pretty calm," Sharon said, giving the sweet bay a gentle rump pat. "I don't suppose that's because his rider's feeling calm?"

Katie stopped brushing for a moment. "You know, it's funny. I've been so busy this morning—getting my clothes ready, grooming Bloop, trying to calm down Matt and Romance—I haven't had time to get nervous yet!" She laughed. "Thanks for reminding me, though, Sharon. There's still plenty of time to panic."

"You have time to watch the lead-line class? They're so cute."

The lead-line participants were the under-seven riders who were brand-new to shows. A counselor accompanied each horse with a lead line as the rider went through very basic moves. It sounded like a good introduction to shows, having a partner in the ring, Katie thought. Too bad she was way too old for that kind of hand-holding.

"I think I'd better pass. When I'm done with Blooper, I want to see if Matt needs any last-minute help."

Just then Jenna and Melissa appeared. Jenna had her little sister, Allegra, on her shoulders. Allegra, who was eight and attended a special school for retarded children, was carrying a riding crop and peering out from underneath Jenna's way-too-big hard hat.

"Look who I found!" Jenna said.

"Legs!" Katie exclaimed, giving her a high-five. "Come to watch your sister ride?"

"I don't care if she wins, though," Allegra said.

"Good thing," Melissa teased, "since I'll be blowing her away in the jumper class."

"You have my permission to whack her with that crop, Legs," Jenna said.

"Are Turbo and Big Red groomed already?" Katie asked as she reached for a mane comb.

"Melissa woke me up at the crack of dawn," Jenna complained. "She had Red ready to go before the sun was up."

"Don't you just love shows?" Melissa said. "Everybody's so excited. It's like Christmas."

"Don't you even get a little nervous?" Katie asked.

"Sure, right before a class. But it passes once you're in the ring. You're so busy trying to concentrate on everything you've learned that you forget about the judges and the spectators and the pressure—"

"Shh!" Sharon warned. "I'm not sure you're helping."

"It's hard to imagine you nervous, Melissa," Katie said as she carefully ran the comb through Blooper's black mane. "You look so calm and confident and . . . not frantic."

"Hey," Melissa said with a wink, "I have a date with destiny today. Anyone watching the lead-line class?"

"I'll go with you," Sharon said. "Let me know if you

need anything, by the way," she added to Katie and Jenna. "I'm playing all-purpose gofer and dorm mom today."

"Thanks, Sharon," Katie said. "You know what I think? I think by our next show, you'll be riding with us."

"No." Sharon shook her head somberly. "By the next show, I'll be *beating* you!"

"Hey," Jenna said, lowering her voice as Sharon and Melissa left. She moved closer so that Allegra could scratch Blooper's ears. "What do you think she meant by *date with destiny?*"

"Probably that she's hoping to win lots of ribbons. You know Melissa."

"You don't think she meant . . . you know—Mr. X?"

"I hope not. What are you going to do about that, anyway, Jen?"

"Here's the plan. I finish my jumper class, then I call the Feds real quick and join the Witness Protection Program. You know—where they change your name and identity?"

Katie laughed. "Brilliant. Yet another glitchless plan."

"I like your name," Allegra argued. "Don't change it."

"I suppose you're right, Legs." Jenna sighed. "Come on. I need to find you a front-row seat before you crush my shoulders into smithereens. You need any help with Bloop, Katie?"

Katie stood back to admire his glossy coat. "Nope. I think I've got everything under control."

"He looks great. You nervous yet?"

"I've been too busy. But I'm sure it's just a matter of time."

"Remember this. We'll be together in the walk/trot class. Think of it as just another class at Silver Creek, you and I having a good time. I'll be right there with you."

"You and a bunch of judges and a million other people."

"Yeah, there's a big crowd, all right. But a million may be a little high. Well, we're off. I'll see you in the warm-up ring soon."

"Bye, Legs," Katie said.

"You don't have to win, either," Legs told her solemnly. "Just don't fall off, okay?"

"Okay." Katie laughed. "I'll try not to."

She watched Jenna and Allegra gallop off. She wondered if her family was here yet. She'd told them not to visit her before the show, since she planned to be a basket case. Still, it would have been nice, in a way, to hear one of her sisters or her brother say what Legs had said. That Katie didn't have to win. That it didn't really matter.

She spent some more time with Blooper, primping and smoothing. He seemed to love the attention, the good old guy. She was lucky to be riding such a well-mannered, experienced horse. How many shows had Blooper been in? she wondered. Dozens, at least.

"I hope I don't let you down, Bloop," she whispered, smoothing down his mane one last time. His red-brown coat caught the sunlight streaming in from the doorway, gleaming like the waxed mahogany dining-room table in Katie's house.

Just then a tall, dark-haired guy, maybe eighteen or so, strode past her purposefully. Although she'd never seen him at the stable before, he seemed to know just where he was going. As he passed Katie, he smiled at her broadly. Instantly she recognized the eyes. They were Matt's eyes—intense and coal-dark. Alec. It had to be.

"Hey, could you rejoin us Earthlings for a minute?"

Matt looked up in surprise to find Katie approaching, her grooming bucket in one hand. "Oh. Hi. I guess you saw me with Alec?"

"I figured he had to be your brother. Either that, or someone's been cloning you without your knowledge."

Matt ran his hand along Romance's back. The mare flinched slightly at his touch. Romance had been like that all morning. Skittish, on edge. Like him, come to think of it.

"Where were you, anyway?" Katie asked.

"What do you mean?" Matt asked.

"I mean, you looked like you were about a zillion miles away just now."

"Actually, if you want to know the truth—" Matt managed a self-deprecating smile. "I was imagining how many different ways I could humiliate myself in the ring. When you caught up with me, I was being thrown clear out of the ring into the muck heap."

Katie laughed. "What brought that horrible fantasy on?"

"Alec, I suppose. He told me he was sure we'd do great, which of course started me thinking how great he always does in shows, which started me thinking how lousy I could do today ... You get the idea."

"What else did he say?" Katie reached for a body brush and began to stroke Romance gently and evenly. The mare practically sighed, as if she were relieved to have her new friend around.

Matt had to admit he was glad to have Katie around, too. Glad he'd been able to get past his own temper and make such a great friend. Whatever happened today at the show, he'd begun to change, and Katie had been the one who'd helped him do it.

"Well," he said, "Alec told me what he does in the show ring is concentrate—equitation, jumping, doesn't matter. He says he tries to stay focused on everything he's learned, and then he just counts on his horse to do the rest. I have to admit, it works for him. He's got a roomful of trophies and ribbons to prove it."

Katie paused to give Romance a little muzzle scratch. "She seems awfully tense today," she commented. "Funny, she's been so much more relaxed lately."

"It's me." Matt clenched his fists in frustration. "I'm tense, so she's tense. Pretty soon I'll blow my top over something, and she'll be biting every entrant in the jumper class."

Katie laughed. "Let's hope not. Jenna's in that class. She'll bite right back." She resumed brushing. "You know, what works for Alec might not work for you, Matt. You said yourself that you and Alec are complete opposites. It seems to me you need to stick to what you've been doing. Stay calm, breathe through those moments when you start to get angry, and relax. Don't think about all the details quite so much."

"And sing 'The Star-Spangled Banner,' right?"

"Well, I'm getting a little tired of your musical selection, but yeah. It seems to be working. Why change now?"

Matt stroked Romance's back. His fingers just grazed Katie's as she brushed. He looked away, suddenly embarrassed, not sure how she would react. "You know, Katie," he said, bending down to retrieve a mane comb so she wouldn't notice the heat in his face, "we've been talking about me all this time. What about you? How are you and Blooper holding up?"

"Bloop's fine. Me, I'm not so sure about. But I feel pretty calm. And I think I have you to thank for that."

"Me?" Matt stood and met her eyes. Her very brown, very pretty eyes.

Katie gave a wide smile. "I'm so busy worrying about you and Romance, I don't have time to worry about me."

"Glad I could be of assistance." Matt laughed, and for the first time all morning the hollow feeling in his stomach evaporated. "Anyway, what's the worst that could happen, right?"

"You could make a total fool of yourself," Katie volunteered.

"Yep. Flying into the muck heap, singing 'The Star-Spangled Banner' as I go."

14

Katie sat on Blooper, waiting to enter the ring for her walk/trot class. Waiting for the panic to hit. Waiting to realize that she should never, ever have listened to her friends and entered this show.

Jenna, her face flushed with excitement, sat nearby on Turbo. Louisa Tisch was whispering last-minute instructions to Escape Route. Bill Weinstein was adjusting his stirrups for the third time in the past five minutes. Altogether there were eleven entrants in the class, none of whom looked anywhere near as nervous as Katie.

Near the show ring entrance, Melissa, Sharon, and Matt were waiting. Matt caught Katie's eye and gave her a thumbs-up.

"I promise you, it'll be fun," Jenna said.

Katie looked over at Jenna. "That's what you said when you talked me into helping you sit for the Klingstedt triplets."

"Hey, it's not my fault they microwaved your English homework."

Katie tensed her grip on her reins and commanded herself to relax. She tried to remember all the good advice she'd given Matt, but her mind was a jumble of images. Scurrying riders. Horses dancing back and forth nervously. And off in the stands, the expectant faces of families and friends.

She started to scan the rows for her family, then stopped herself. It would be better if she didn't see them, better if she didn't think about disappointing them.

"Riders for the walk/trot class, prepare to enter." Rose's voice echoed in Katie's ears. "And have fun!"

Katie forced a smile. This *was* just a summer camp show, she reminded herself, not the Olympic trials.

One of the counselors motioned for them to enter the show ring. Katie moved Blooper into line behind Jenna and Turbo. Jenna looked back and gave her a grin. "Remember, *fun*."

"Fun," Katie repeated dully.

They entered the show ring and came to a halt, waiting for the judge's first instruction. "Riders," Claire said into the microphone, "please begin by walking your horses in a circle, clockwise."

Katie gave Blooper a gentle nudge of her legs behind the girth, pushing her hips into the saddle. As soon as he responded, she relaxed her legs and checked her position. It should have been easy, old hat, and yet she felt her back and shoulders tensing, her hands clutching the reins too tightly. She could feel the eyes boring into her. Teachers, counselors . . . family.

Seconds ticked by. Ahead of her, Jenna and Turbo looked absolutely at home with each other. Why couldn't Katie relax the same way? It was just a simple walk, the easiest thing in the world to master.

"Riders, please begin a rising trot," Claire instructed, "continuing clockwise."

As Katie signaled Blooper to trot, she whispered, "Correct diagonal, Katie, remember your diagonal." She felt the familiar two-beat gait beneath her and began to post correctly, but somehow she couldn't seem to relax into the movement. Her lower legs were flapping as she rose to post, her hands were bobbing. In her mind, she could hear Margaret barking corrections at her.

She wondered if her family could tell she was blowing it. Her eyes strayed for just a split second to the stands, and then she saw them—her father, her stepmother, John, Natalie, Elise. Elise was holding something, a small piece of cardboard.

Katie yanked her eyes away. That kind of distraction could cost her points, she knew. She needed to concentrate, and yet when she came around the far side of the ring, she couldn't help taking one more quick glance. She scanned the stands until she located the sign Elise was holding.

WE LOVE YOU, KATIE! it said.

In some part of her mind, Katie heard Claire call for a serpentine at a trot. She would have to remember to change diagonals. She would have to remember lots of things to even have a chance at a ribbon.

But she knew when the show was over, what she'd remember most was the little cardboard sign in her sister's hands.

"Fourth place your first show," Sharon said, gazing admiringly at Katie's white ribbon. She and Katie were standing near the entrance to the show ring, waiting for the jumper class, the final class of the day, to start.

"Well, Blooper deserves a lot of the credit," Katie said, leaning against the fence with a sigh. "You know, the ribbon doesn't even matter. I'm just so proud I actually went through with it. The truth is, I didn't even realize Claire had called my name until I saw my family jumping up and down in the stands."

"Last, but most definitely not least, the jumper class will begin momentarily," Rose announced. "We're all rooting for you, guys! First rider, Jenna McCloud on Turbo."

"Rose has a very original announcing style," Sharon said, grinning.

"I don't know who to root for," Katie said, "with Jenna, Melissa, and Matt all competing."

"My guess is Matt and Melissa will both place— depending, that is, on how Matt and Romance are getting along," Sharon said. "Jenna might, too, although most of the others have a lot more experience."

"She was so excited about taking the second in walk/trot, she told me she'll be happy as long as she doesn't fall off Turbo," Katie said.

Sharon shielded her eyes from the bright sun. "It's a fairly straightforward jump course, nothing fancy. She'll have a good round. You want to worry about anyone, worry about Romance. I thought she seemed awfully skittish in the stable this morning when Matt was grooming her."

"I just talked to Matt in the warm-up ring a few minutes ago to tell him good luck. Romance seemed calmer after he took her over a few practice jumps to get her suppled up. Matt, I'm not so sure about."

They watched as Jenna entered the ring and urged Turbo into a springy, collected canter. They took the first jump, a short vertical, flawlessly, but Jenna turned Turbo a little late into the oxer that followed. He took off at an angle, losing some of his momentum.

"That's hard," Sharon commented. "The moment you land one fence, the approach to the next one starts. You need to be thinking ahead all the time. When you cut corners like that, you lose impulsion."

"There's so much to remember," Katie said, watching in admiration as Jenna and Turbo made their way through the rest of the course. No wonder Matt was so anxious.

"It gets easier with practice," Sharon assured her. "Like everything. And it helps when you have a horse who really loves to jump like Turbo. Jenna's right about him. He's going to be one heck of a jumper someday."

Jenna finished her course and the girls burst into applause. "Nice job," Sharon said. "No serious faults."

"She looked great to me," Katie said, "but then, I'm not a judge."

Two riders later, they heard Rose call Melissa's name. "Next rider," the loudspeaker boomed, "Melissa Hall on Big Red."

Watching Melissa and Big Red flow around the course with seemingly effortless grace, Katie could begin to see what the judges must be looking for. She approached each jump with a smooth, even stride, never rushing, never slowing, taking off at precisely the right distance. She traced beautiful, fluid arcs over each obstacle as if she and Big Red were one animal.

"She makes it look so easy," Katie whispered.

"That's the trick," Sharon said, nodding. "Melissa's one of the best."

Katie thought she heard a catch in Sharon's voice. She turned to look at her friend and was surprised to see tears in Sharon's eyes.

"You'll be out there next time," Katie said, patting her shoulder. "I'm sure of it, Sharon."

"You know, it's not the ribbons I miss," Sharon said. "It's Cass. Sometimes . . ." She cleared her throat and shrugged, and in a transforming instant she was the old, confident Sharon again. "I guess I'll never stop missing her," she said matter-of-factly.

"That's good, Sharon. You don't want to ever forget a horse like Cassidy."

"A friend like Cassidy," Sharon corrected.

Melissa finished her round to a burst of applause. "Red put in an extra stride on that last vertical,"

Sharon said as she clapped furiously. "But I think Melissa has a shot at the blue. Keep your fingers crossed."

They watched seven more riders, only one of whom seemed to be a threat to Melissa. "Winnie could take first," Sharon conceded. "It was a flawless round, but personally, I liked Melissa's style better. Winnie really muscles her horse through the course. You have to be aggressive, but jumping is supposed to be beautiful, too."

"And our final rider today in the jumper class," came Rose's booming voice, "will be Matt Collier."

"Poor Matt," Katie said, gripping the fence tightly. "He's probably a bundle of nerves by now. Which means Romance is probably a very large bundle of nerves by now."

Sharon gazed at Katie, pursing her lips.

"What?" Katie asked.

"I was just trying to decide. Is it the horse you're worried about or the rider?"

"Both," Katie admitted.

"You like this guy, huh?"

Fortunately, Katie didn't have time to answer, because just then Matt and Romance took off at a brisk canter.

"Beautiful," Sharon murmured after the first jump. "Absolutely perfect."

Katie didn't have time to watch for fine points of technique. She was too busy trying to catch a glimpse of Matt's face. Romance, at least, appeared to be having a wonderful time, bounding over the jumps as if they weren't there. *Her* face was all concentrated joy.

But Matt's face was obscured by his hard hat. It wasn't until he and Romance made a perfect, wide arc in preparation for a triple that Katie could finally get a clear look.

He wasn't just smiling. He was singing.

"I know this sounds crazy," Sharon whispered, "but did I just hear the words *rocket's red glare?*"

A few minutes later Katie watched as Rose walked over to hand Matt his third-place ribbon. She wasn't sure whom she was prouder of—Matt or Romance. As Rose moved closer to Romance, she winked at Matt. "She seems to be on her best behavior today," Rose said, "so I guess I don't have anything to worry about."

Just then, Romance nudged Rose with her muzzle, then lipped a mouthful of her hair. Katie caught her breath. "No, Romance," she whispered. "Behave." To her amazement—and Rose's, apparently—Romance didn't pull. She just let go of Rose's hair and gave a little self-congratulatory head dip.

"That's my girl," Rose exclaimed. She reached into her pocket, pulled out another ribbon, and presented it to Romance.

While the crowd laughed and applauded, Romance sniffed the ribbon, considered eating it, then gave another little nod, as if to bow. Matt took the ribbon from Rose and held it up for Katie to see.

When all the ribbons had been announced, Katie headed off for her locker. Not bad, not bad at all. It had been a good day for the Silver Creek Riders. A second for Jenna, plus a sixth in the jumper class. A fourth for Katie. And a second for Melissa. Not only that, but Matt and Romance had come through with flying colors.

When she'd retrieved the present she'd hidden in her locker for Matt, she went to Romance's stall to wait for him. He arrived a few minutes later, looking relieved and happy. Romance looked like she couldn't wait for her next show to start.

"Hey, I've been looking for you," Matt said as he began to untack Romance. "I just ran into Alec."

"What'd he say?" Katie asked.

"He asked me what my secret was." Matt shook his head. "I told him 'The Star-Spangled Banner,' and he just looked confused." He reached over and retrieved the yellow ribbon on Romance's bridle. "Here," he said. "This really belongs to you."

"No. It's Romance's," Katie said.

"She wants you to have it. Besides, if you don't take it, she may lose her willpower and eat it."

"Okay, then. I'll trade you." Katie took the ribbon and handed Matt her gift, a rolled-up piece of paper tied with a string.

Matt unfurled the paper and gasped. "It's Romance and me, going over a jump. Katie, it's—" Suddenly he frowned. "No, it's not quite right, actually."

"What?" Katie asked anxiously. "Don't you like it?"

"It's just . . . well, you have me in perfect form."

Katie laughed with relief. "Artistic license, that's called. But you like it?"

Matt shook his head slowly, wonderingly. "I more than like it," he said.

He looked at her shyly. She felt his hand slip into hers. Their fingers entwined easily.

No mittens necessary.

15

Melissa stood in the tack room and checked her watch. Ten minutes since the awards ceremony for the last class, and still no Mr. X.

She held her shiny red ribbon up and grinned at it. Not blue, true. But not bad.

It surprised her that she hadn't minded losing the blue to Winnie. She'd been preparing for this show with such high hopes. She'd thought taking a first would be a nice symbolic end to camp, a way of saying yes, she could make it here. She hadn't wanted to move here, she hadn't wanted to attend Silver Creek. She was isolated because of her race. She'd lost her boyfriend, and still, yes, Melissa Hall, tough-as-they-come Melissa, had made it all work. Like her mom always said, if you put your mind to it, you can do anything.

But when Claire had called her name for second place, something had happened. She'd ridden Big Red up to the judges' stand, and while Claire had clipped the red ribbon to his bridle—the ribbon that was *supposed* to be blue—Melissa had realized that somebody was screaming her name. Three somebodies, in fact— Sharon and Katie and Jenna. She'd turned to see them applauding and leaping and just generally making complete fools of themselves. And at that moment, the color of her ribbon had simply ceased to matter.

Melissa checked her watch again. She wondered how long she should wait. The post-show party by the lake would be starting soon. Rose had promised plenty of munchies, which was a good thing, since Melissa was famished. It was always that way. Before a show, she could never eat. Afterward, she could eat her weight in food.

She glanced out of the tack-room door. A few more minutes, then she'd chalk this up to a lost cause. Just then the phone on the wall began to ring. Melissa hesitated. It was, after all, just for emergencies. She'd never actually heard it ring before.

Three, four, five rings. Well, someone had to get it, and she was the only one around. She picked up the receiver cautiously. "Hello?"

"Melissa?" The voice was low, hoarse, and muffled, like a frog talking into a pillow.

"Um, yes. This is Melissa Hall. Who's this?"

"You don't know?"

"Kermit the frog?"

"It is I. Mr. X."

"Mr. X! I didn't think . . . I was starting to be afraid it was all some kind of silly joke. But you're real."

"Of course I'm real. I'm as real as the moon. I'm as real as the stars. I'm as real as . . ." A long pause. "I'm as real as . . . well, real things."

Melissa wrapped the cord around her finger. "I thought you were going to—" She paused when Louisa came in to drop off a bridle. "I thought you were going to come see me," she whispered when Louisa was gone.

"Well, that's why I'm calling. You see, I have—" There was a pause for several loud coughs. "I have a terrible, highly contagious disease, as perhaps you can tell. It's called . . . actually, the doctors aren't sure yet. But they know it's highly contagious."

"That's awful! When did you come down with this?"

"This morning. They rushed me away. I had to miss the show."

"I wondered where you were. I listened for them to call your name in all the classes. I asked around, but no one seemed to know you."

"As I may have mentioned, I'm very shy."

Melissa sighed heavily. "But couldn't I come to see you?"

"No!" It was almost a scream. "I mean, no. You couldn't risk it, dear Melissa."

"But for true love," Melissa persisted, "you do anything. That's how the legend of Comet and Aurora ends, after all."

"It is?" The voice registered real surprise. "I mean, you *know* the legend?"

"Sure. Everybody who loves horses has heard it."

"So, um, how does it . . . which ending did you hear, exactly? There are different versions, you know."

"Mr. X," Melissa said, "can you hold on for just a minute? I mean, you're not on death's doorstep or anything, are you?"

"No, but you might say I'm in his driveway."

"I'll be quick. I just thought I heard some commotion in the barn and I want to go check it out. I'll be right back, promise."

Melissa let the phone dangle. She reached for her ribbon and the piece of notebook paper she'd tucked into her hard hat. Then she ran out of the tack room into the sunny afternoon.

Jenna hugged the receiver to her chest. "She ran to the stable," she explained. "She heard some noise. You think she's buying the handkerchief act?"

"You sound like Kermit the frog," Sharon said.

"Yeah, I heard that somewhere. I hope she comes back soon," Jenna muttered, checking to see if Melissa had returned. "Rose said we could just use the office phone for a few minutes."

"Here's what I don't get," Katie said. "How come she knows the ending to the legend when *we* don't even know the ending to the legend?"

Jenna put the receiver to her ear again and positioned the handkerchief. "Melissa, dear?" she croaked as Katie and Sharon gathered close to listen.

"I'm back, Mr. X," Melissa said sweetly. "Just don't breathe on me with those nasty nameless germs, okay?"

"How come this connection is so much clearer all of a sudden?" Jenna asked. "You sound like you're—"

Someone tapped Jenna on the shoulder. "In the same room?"

Jenna spun around, tossing the phone into the air. "Melissa!"

"Melissa!" Katie cried.

"Melissa!" Sharon repeated.

"Mr. X, I presume?" Melissa sat down in a chair, arms crossed over her chest.

"You knew?" Jenna demanded, hanging up the phone. "How long?"

"Since, oh, I don't know, around the first line of your first letter."

"My handwriting." Jenna pounded her palm against her forehead. "I thought if I wrote with my left hand, you wouldn't be able to recognize it."

"I wouldn't have, either. Except you're the only one I know who dots her *i*'s with a circle. Dead giveaway."

"But why didn't you say something?" Sharon asked. She grinned. "Oh, never mind. I can answer that one. You were having too much fun setting up Jenna."

Jenna groaned. "I'm really sorry, Melissa. It sort of got out of hand. We were just trying to make you feel better."

"You did." Melissa grinned.

"We did?"

"Sure. I realized how lucky I am to have friends who care enough about me to make complete idiots of themselves." Melissa gazed at the ribbon in her hand. "I have been preoccupied lately, I know, what with Marcus and the show. But today I realized when I came in second that I'd rather have you three than a blue ribbon anyday. Well, okay, I'd rather have you guys *and* a blue ribbon. But this is pretty great." She passed a piece of paper to Jenna. "Sorry," she said. "I can't fold horses."

"What's this?" Jenna asked.

Melissa smiled. "The end of the legend, of course."

Jenna unfolded the note. "Dear Mr. X," she read.

I am writing what will be our last letter, but it wouldn't be fair to say good-bye without finishing the legend of Comet and Aurora as I heard it recounted.

When last we saw the poor old guy, Comet was standing on the bank of the raging Silver River, holding his declaration of love written by Mariah. On the other side of the river, gazing back longingly, was beautiful Aurora.

At last Comet could stand it no more. He took the letter between his teeth and jumped into the wild, churning rapids of the icy river. He struggled with all his strength against the horrendous current, but though he was the mightiest of stallions, he could not make it to the other side.

Aurora, watching in horror as Comet was swept away, didn't hesitate for a moment. She leapt into the river to save Comet, but the torrent grabbed her just as it had taken Comet. Together they were dragged against their will down the river. Aurora swam with all her·might until she reached Comet's side. And at that very moment, they were sucked down into a huge whirlpool, never to be seen again.

Mariah, touched by their display of courage and love, turned both horses to stone. Even today, in the gentle remains of the Silver River that we now know as Silver Creek, you can see them together, two granite rocks, side by side, parting the current forever.

"Wow," Katie said, sniffling. "What a great story. But it's so sad. Couldn't you have had a happy ending?"

Melissa shrugged. "It's a legend. It's supposed to be poignant."

"I sure am glad you came up with an ending," Jenna said. "Because I was just going to say something like 'They lived happily ever after. Don't ask me for details, use your imagination.'" She sighed. "But I'm kind of sorry to see old Mr. X bite the dust. He was quite the romantic writer."

"Actually, he was pretty nauseating, Jen," Melissa said.

"Besides," Sharon added with a grin, "he was highly contagious."

"I am not walking one foot unless you load me into a wheelbarrow and push," Jenna said firmly early that evening as the post-show party began to wind down. "I ate three and a half hot dogs."

"Four and a half," Katie corrected. "But who's counting?"

"Look, McCloud," Sharon warned, "I put up with your insane letter-writing idea. You can walk a few hundred yards for one of mine." She checked her watch. "Come on. We have to hurry."

"I just don't get why we have to do it now," Jenna whined.

"She just wants to take Luna for a walk in the pasture," Melissa said.

"But why?"

Sharon grabbed Jenna's right arm and Katie grabbed her left. "One, two, three, heave!" Sharon commanded, lurching Jenna into a more-or-less upright position.

The four girls headed to the stable and harnessed up Luna, who was her usual unenthusiastic self. "Who were you on the phone with before, Sharon?" Katie asked.

"The phone?" Sharon asked nonchalantly.

"You know. Makes little ringy noises, has buttons with numbers?" Jenna prompted.

"Oh. Just Mr. Hardesty."

"Mr. Hardesty," Melissa repeated. "Why Mr. Hardesty?"

"Look," Sharon said as she led Luna out of the stable. "I don't want to tell you why, because I've already been wrong once, and if I'm wrong about this, too, I'll never hear the end of it. Especially not from Jenna, since I've been needling her endlessly about *her* stupid idea."

"You're not still thinking she misses that gelding, are you?" Katie asked as they headed toward the west paddock.

"No, I'm not," Sharon said. "I'm thinking she misses . . . someone else."

"Another gelding?"

"No."

"A mare?"

"No," Sharon said shortly.

"You don't think she made friends with that little mule of his, do you?" Katie asked. "Because I've heard of horses who'll do that, you know—"

"If you must know." Sharon stopped in her tracks. "I'm thinking she's missing Arthur."

"Arthur? Is that one of Mr. Hardesty's kids?"

"No." Sharon buried her face in Luna's neck. "He's one of his beagles."

"Excuse me?" Jenna said, grinning in disbelief. "Your latest theory is that Luna is lovesick for a *beagle*?"

Sharon pulled on Luna's lead rope gently and they resumed their walk. "It could happen."

"Yeah," Melissa said. "And pigs will be flying anyday now."

"Look, all I know is that in that picture of yours, Luna was having fun with something small and brown. And remember when we were at the Hardestys' farm, and Mr. Hardesty mentioned he had a beagle puppy he kept on a leash because the puppy was chasing the cows all over the place?"

"But that sounds like the kind of dog who'd scare Luna to death," Katie pointed out.

"Yeah, except Claire told me Luna's owner has a bunch of dogs. Plus, let's face it, she's kind of a strange character, anyway."

They reached the pasture gate. Jenna unlatched it and Sharon led Luna through. "So we're going to watch a rendezvous between a beagle and a filly. This oughtta be good." Jenna rubbed her hands together. "I'm going to hate saying I told you so, Sharon. Although—" She looked at Luna and sighed. "Never mind. I take that back. I'd give anything to see Luna back to her old self."

"You never know," Katie said. "Animals can make odd friends. I once had a cat who slept with a guinea pig."

"Well, maybe the cat slept," Sharon said. "I doubt the guinea pig got a real good night's sleep."

Halfway down the pasture, they paused. The sun was making a glorious, copper-colored exit. Sharon unclipped Luna's lead rope and took a step back. Luna looked at her with sad, listless eyes. "I hope this isn't crazy," Sharon whispered to her.

Fifty yards down the fence, in a clearing between deep piles of brush, Mr. Hardesty appeared. He leaned over the fence and waved. The girls waved back. "But where's Arthur?" Katie asked.

Suddenly a flash of brown whizzed over the fence and rocketed toward the girls, yelping hysterically, paws barely touching the ground.

Sharon gulped. Had she made a terrible mistake? This dog looked like a high-speed train. What if Luna was terrified?

But as Arthur neared, Luna's ears perked up, her tail flicked, her whole body went on alert. Arthur turned in a wide arc, barking frantically as he aimed right for Luna's hind feet.

"No!" Sharon cried, reaching to pull Luna out of

harm's way, but just then Luna tossed back her head and let out a whinny of pure, unadulterated joy. Just in the nick of time she galloped off, hooves thundering. Dog and horse wove and danced, Arthur leaping up to yap a greeting, Luna bending down to give him a playful nudge. It was like a strange cross-species ballet, a dance they'd clearly danced many times before.

"Amazing," Sharon whispered. "She really *is* a lunatic."

"But now she's a happy one," Katie added.

"Guess you were right," Mr. Hardesty said as the girls walked over to join him at the fence. "But I have to admit it was the craziest darn theory I'd heard in some time. You'd think that filly'd be scared to death of that crazy hound."

"She's pretty crazy herself," Sharon said. "I don't suppose we could work out some kind of visitation arrangement?"

"You better believe it," Mr. Hardesty said with a wink. "I've never seen Arthur so happy."

While Luna and Arthur danced and frolicked, the girls watched the sun disappear behind a low ridge of dark hills. The breeze carried the softest touch of autumn, the cool scent of sweaters and school.

"It's starting to feel like the end of summer," Katie said. "I'm going to hate to see camp end."

"Yeah," Sharon said. "No more mosquito bites. No more peeling noses."

"No more riding every single day," Jenna said sadly, "living and breathing horses."

The girls fell silent, watching Luna amble through the grass with her friend.

"But the Silver Creek Riders will still be around," Katie said firmly.

Melissa grinned. "The legend continues."